THE
WHORE
HOUSE
THAT
JACK
BUILT

By Kevin Sweeney

For

KEVIN SWEENEY

PUBLISHER'S NOTE:

MorbidbookS is a grotesque Bizarro ballet where the most profane things occur. An impious and perverse dwelling of dark revulsion. A cozy cottage where torture porn and brutal bible tales are devised. A quiet place to relax and spin tales of depravity and wickedness. A halfway house for the disturbed where rules no longer apply. A safe haven for deviant serial killers to hatch their wretched schemes. Bring your pets.
The tasty ones are always welcome.

HTTPS://WWW.MORBIDBOOKS.WORDPRESS.COM

KEVIN SWEENEY

AUTHOR'S NOTE.

Django. The Quick and the Dead. Blood Meridian. Some of
the inspiration for writing this book.
And porn, of course.

PROLOGUE

Nowhere, Undiscovered Country, 1899

He approached the door of the whorehouse and felt his cock stir
alive like a rattlesnake rearing up and giving a warning shake of its
tail and at his side his dog Lady whined and that stiffened his cock
even more but tonight well tonight he wouldn't be fucking his dog.

Clem Tumblety had come a long and hard trail and now
stood in a kind of religious awe. He'd heard tell of Musselmen who
once in their lives had to make a trip to be a big black stone, a stone
called "Mekka", and he would calculate that the way he felt now
stood in the dooryard of the whorehouse was how those
Musselmen felt when they finally reach that big black stone.

Lady at his side whined again.

"Hush up now, ol' gel," Clem told his faithful smell-hound,
and he knelt down on one complaining knee with a wince to stroke
her patchy fur, "This here is it. We done everythin' that ol' nigger
done said ta do, and by God here we is."

THE WHOREHOUSE THAT JACK BUILT

Lady whined again.

Clem had owned her since she was a puppy, had traded two plugs of tobacco for her at some split in the road whose name he'd long forgot. She was more loyal than a brother and more faithful than any piece of cunny. He smiled down into her old face now, at her drooling toothless mouth; she was drooling because she was nervous, and she was toothless because that was the whole reason he'd bought her.

Clem had made a scratch living trapping, and that meant living away from what folk called civilization and he liked that just fine. But it got lonely hunting out on the prairies, in the mountains. At night a man needed comfort.

When she was a pup he'd fed Lady a little whiskey and when she was passed out he had pulled every tooth from her head. She couldn't fight or hunt after that, but by God she could make a man come hard, could lick and slobber your cock with her big old wet-rough tongue until you shot your fuck hissing into the fire six feet away, just like whipping a snake by the tail so as his brains shot out his mouth.

Now here they were, stood outside a whorehouse in a ghost town, and it was the end.

"G'night ol' gel," said Clem.

Lady licked his hand and gave a hopeful wag of her tail. Her tail was a stump, because sometimes he wanted some tight hole action and a tail got in the way. On those days he'd feed her chicken guts, because chicken guts didn't agree with Lady and she'd spend the whole night shitting and shitting, which lubricated her asshole just right for Clem to pretend he was fucking a tight little Chink.

When Clem was younger and had spare coin and found himself in the locale of a hog ranch he always asked after a celestial; Chinks were tiny, and their cunts and assholes were nearly tight enough to clip a man's cock off like a snapping turtle.

He patted Lady's head. She nuzzled his fingers.

"I love you, gel," he said, and broke her neck.

He laid her gently on the ground amongst the scattered fortune discarded at the whorehouse door, coins and bills shored up like drifts of leaves.

In his head the old nigger said, *once you go through the door, you ain't comin' back out. Best t'tek care a' yours afore you step in.*

He'd met the old nigger whilst he was busy getting himself on the outside of a bottle of forty rod. This was in Spurlock, a once Hell-on-Wheels town long ago that had been a hoot but had gotten itself civilized after the war, as the last vestiges of the Frontier receded. He'd come to town because he could no longer ignore the pain in his belly or the blood in his shit.

He was getting drunk because the doctor had given him weeks to live. Said he had a canker, a tumour as big as a 'coons head spreading evil roots through his guts. He'd prescribed heroin for the pain and prayer for the preparation of Clem's soul, though the way Clem figured the matter, in his sixty four years of life he hadn't done much to put him in St Peter's favour... quite the other way, in fact.

So he hit a saloon and bought a bottle and got to drinking the pain away and next thing there's this old nigger sat in a corner under a colour lithograph of "Custer's Last Fight" provided by the Anheuser & Busch Brewing Company, asking and answering a question;

Y'all ever hear of the Half-World? But a'course you ain't.

Clem didn't even know he was being spoken to.

Nobody hears of the Half-World until they cross the border of the Undiscovered Country. And you only just set your foot into that country, didn't you Mr Tumblety?

That had got Clem's attention.

How d'you know my name, nigger?

And that was how it started, with an old, blind nigger speaking his name without ever having met him.

A'course the old, blind nigger was not blind or a nigger. That was just the skin that the thing happened to be wearing. Clem figured the old nigger wasn't human part ways from what it spoke of, from the fact that it was openly petitioning for his soul, and the fact that twice as they talked something like the eye stalks of slugs each as long and thick as a man's trigger-finger flowed out of the old niggers nostrils to blink shining golden eyes at him.

And what the thing in the old nigger's flesh spoke of was the Half-World.

It was a whorehouse, but not one open to just anyone. To get there you had to be dying or insane. The services offered were all offered for the same price, which was everything you had. There were paths there that only those who had crossed the border into the Undiscovered Country could find, if they knew the landmarks to follow, the signs to watch for.

Clem followed and watched and two days ago his mule had done died of exhaustion and it was just him and Lady keepin' on who knew how and finally they came to a dead town with no name at twilight and a whorehouse with a sign above the door that Clem could not read:

A SOILED DOVE IN A CAGE

PUTS ALL HEAVEN IN A RAGE

A whorehouse run by demons. A whorehouse that offered the greatest pleasures a man could ever want... in exchange for everything he had.

Am I gonna do this? Am I really gonna...

The cancer in his belly twisted spikes through his impacted bowels and in front of him lay Lady, a sacrifice.

And Clem pushed that door open and stepped across the threshold.

*

(not human none of 'em)

The difference between the dying and the insane was that the insane were ready for what waited within the Half-World. But the spell of time between stepping through the front door of the whorehouse and stepping through the bedroom door of the whore he had chosen was all a blur for Clem, and when he saw what was waiting on the bed almost everything he had seen was forgotten. A mind can do such things; a mind sometimes has to.

THE WHOREHOUSE THAT JACK BUILT

He forgot

(hundreds and hundreds of miles and miles of wood and buildings)

meeting the dwarf, forgot the "possibles" in the parlour

(their eyes they all had those eyes)

Almost forgot about what he had seen downstairs as now he looked upon his ultimate fantasy.

She stood up from the silk sheeted bed and bowed at the waist, her hands together in front like she was setting to say her prayers.

Clem barely knew what to do with himself. His cock did though, yes sir, that old boy started getting himself nice and swollen and hard.

She was a daughter of Joy, a celestial; both were ways of saying she was a Chink whore, the tiniest slitty eyed Chink whore he'd ever seen. Barely four foot tall, tiny as a child, she wore a lily silk gown that fell around her body in a way that told you she was naked under there. Her face was severe and delicate, her mouth a lotus bud and her eyes

(like theirs oh Gawd what was wrong with their)

and she had those weird feet Clem loved so much. Chink women seemed to think that tiny feet were the fanciest things, and when they were babies their mommas would bind their feet up so the bones didn't grow right, turned them into stumpy trotters the size of fists. Clem loved those messed up feet. But her size, her beauty, and even her feet weren't the most striking thing...

The most striking thing about her was her hair; her head was scraped bald except for a braided pigtail that Clem thought only men Chinks had. Chinks always ran the laundry's in town, and you only ever saw that bald head and pigtail on the men. Hers had to be damn near fifteen foot long. She had been lying on the bed when Clem stepped in with her hair coiled behind her like a snake on the sheets, and when she had got up to receive him that coil had paid out behind her.

"Greetings most honoured guest, and welcome to my chamber."

Clem raised a grimy eyebrow. High class Chink whore had her language all smoothed out, all her "r" and "l" sounds coming out right.

"Wel, *gleetings* and *werrcome* yerself darlin'," said Clem, thinking his humour charming, "You must be good, earnin' enough to be able to pay for *elec-tro-cution* lessons 'nall."

All the strangeness suddenly didn't matter, what he had seen already in the Half-World forgotten, the fact that he was never leaving dismissed from mind. Now there was just Clem and the most toothsome little piece of Chink cunt he had ever seen.

"Please, Mr Tumblety, I wish to bathe you," she said, and with a graceful, stylised motion of her hand she indicated a copper bath across the room stood in front of a black lacquered screen, full of water which steamed slightly, "For your pleasure."

Some whores could be fussy. Mind... Clem pinched the front of his bib and took a whiff. Pole-cat, and long-time dead too; well, a bath'd be a treat.

"Well okay darlin'," he said, "I'll allow that I'm a mite ripe. You gonna scrub me pink 'n' shiny from asshole to appetite?"

THE WHOREHOUSE THAT JACK BUILT

She smiled a small, perfect smile and made a graceful gesture towards the bath again.

Grinning, Clem started shrugging off his clothes... or peeling them off at least. The Chink whore helped him as he went, her fist like feet somehow spirit silent and sure, and her hands ghost butterflies that helped slide his filth stiffened trail clothes off as if they were no more effort to remove then the breath-thin skin of an onion. Clem stopped struggling and let her do the work, and by the time he placed one crusty foot into the bath somehow the whore had stripped him bare.

She helped lower him in nice and slow, her hands under his armpits all of a sudden. For a moment Clem was surprised, wondering how someone so slight could be so strong, but then the oils and creams in the hot water slid across his grubby flesh and bore the thought away before it could settle.

The hot water was so good. He felt his muscles unwinding, tight cords easing, knots being loosened. He groaned.

"Unnh, uhh, oh darlin', that's sumthin' alright', that really is sumthin'..."

Clem's eyes were closed. Tiny hands slid onto his shoulders and kneaded them.

"Relax, honoured guest, relax. Let Fuk Yu take care of you."

Clem chuckled.

"That you'r name, Fuk Yu? Naw, not tonigh' darlin', tonigh' you're goin' to be... Lady. And I am gonna *fuck yoooouuuuu...*"

A hand dipped into the water and brought scoopfuls up to pour down Clem's body.

"Please, and then tell *Lady* what honored guest will do to her," the whore murmured in his ear.

"I'm gonna fuck you, whore. I'mma pound you so hard you'll never walk right again. I'mma give you everythin' I got. I'mma split you, make you bleed, make you beg me to stop poundin' my huge cock into your tight little slit."

"Whatever honored guest wants. Everything tonight is for him."

Because there will not be another. Honoured guest will not see another night.

Clem, eyes still closed, frowned. He didn't know what 'subtext' meant, but he knew it when he heard it. The unpleasant reminder was there that he had

(price, every drop of seed and blood and marrow)

agreed the ultimate price for

(ecstasy they know not even in Heaven)

this.

One of Fuk Yu's hands slid down over his belly, slid down right over where the doctor had told Clem the tumour was growing, like a rotten potato sending out tuber growths into the rest of his guts, making it hard for him to ever take a shit, meaning he was always constipated. For a second there was heat, incredible heat... and then the gnawing pain which had become the background of his life for the past year was gone.

The hand slid lower and cupped his balls, hefted them. That hand was so tiny he didn't fit into it, spilled out. He felt huge in that hand, and in a moment his cock was stone-stiff.

"Uhhn..." he moaned.

"Yes, oh, most honoured one; you are so big, so strong, so male..."

Her hand gently squeezed one of his balls and then the other, unable to cup them both together, and then travelled up along the bottom of his shaft in soft strokes, like her fingers were paint brushes.

She murmured in Chinese into his ear as she began to wash his hair, that sing-song talk he loved to hear, though usually it would be gasped begging he could choose to mean anything as he pounded into a tiny little Chink whore.

At his crotch her hand began to twine around his cock, and Clem had no idea how she was doing it, how her fingers –like paint brushes, horse hair brushes- twisted around and around his shaft, but it was a feeling like none other and he just sank into it.

(washing your hair)

Yeah, warm water running across his itchy scalp, fingers working up dead skin and trail dirt mixed with sweat that had dried and formed crusts at the roots of his thin iron and silver hair.

She was wrapped around his cock and gently, gently squeezing, starting to pull so slow it almost wasn't happening.

(your hair)

Her hands running through it, gently pulling through knots.

And playing with his stiffy at the same time.

What in Hell...

Clem opened his eyes.

Fuk Yu's fingers continued to massage his scalp, scooping up water to wash through it. Both her hands were at his head. He stared down at what was fooling with his genitals.

Around and around the copper bath a black snake had coiled, rearing up over the side to dip into the water, into his lap, where it was curling around and around his red bulbed meat. Its head split into five equal lengths, and Clem realized why it felt so good, like paint brushes... the snake was the coiled length of the Chink's huge *queue* ponytail, which was moving on its own, a serpent-tentacle made of hair.

"Sweet Jesus..." he whispered

(has no place HERE)

The braided length of the ponytail split at the end into a star shape; this star was what gently tugged and squeezed him like paintbrushes.

Clem's mind was suddenly very clear. It was as if his mind had been cocooned, like a fly in a web wrapped up for the spider's larder... and now it was dinner time. He'd been in a fugue since the doctor had first spoke his death sentence, had first become a pilgrim in the Undiscovered Country.

Had he been sleep walking this whole time? Had he really met that nigger who wasn't a nigger... had he wandered the prairies by moonlight with madness singing from the cold and empty sky... to a ghost town called Nowhere and a whorehouse filled with...

Clem had never been a spiritual man. He was a man who lived in nature, understood how blood ran beneath the hot surface of life, fuelled muscle, how everything was just appetite lashed together with bones and veins. He was a hunter, a skinner, a pelt trader. But now he felt himself to be more than just meat.

He had a soul and he'd sold it.

Inside he ran cold, cold, cold.

His cock shrank.

"O, what is this?" murmured the Chink whore in his ear, a note of mockery there in her voice, "Where is the huge cock that *Lady* was promised? Honoured guest promised to make *Lady* bleed, make her beg for him to stop..."

"I," Clem said, and somehow his mouth was dry, so dry he could barely speak, "I don't, I can't..."

Move you fool, run fer it!

Wild hope, but the thought wasn't even full formed in his mind before Clem Tumblety had flung himself from the copper tub and was skittering on his hands and knees away, stumbling to his feet with his eyes on the bedroom door.

He might have been old, but you didn't survive out on the prairies and mountains without reflexes slick as a coyote's. Clem kicked through his own discarded clothes, keeping low and focussed only on the door, never glancing back.

In moments his hand was on the cut glass door knob.

He twisted.

Locked.

Seeing as though the animal part of his brain was in charge he tried again, and again, rattled and shook the door all he could. He kicked at it, punched it, hurt his foot and his hand.

Then he just sort of stopped. The fight went out of him, all at once.

He stared at the varnished wood of the door.

The last thought he had that made any sense, as something curled around his ankle, something warm and rough and smooth all at once, like hemp rope, was an apology; *I'm sorry ol' gel. You was the best mutt I ever had. An' I traded you for a pig in a poke.*

The ponytail coiled once, twice, tightened with a snap and then yanked his leg out from under him like a lasso. Clem cried out as he was unbalanced and toppled to the ground, smacking his face on the door panel as he went, then shutting up when his jaw hit the floor and his teeth clacked together, biting off the tip of his tongue.

Clem felt floorboards under him, then the edge of the rug. He was being pulled along like a roped steer. He grabbed out at anything, snatching at the tasselled edge of the rug, snatched a handful, but all that did was pull the rug up, pulled it with him as he was reeled in.

He kicked and thrashed and that got him nowhere. He ended up on his back and finally ended up looking at what was happening to him.

Fuk Yu was moving soft and smooth on her tiny warped feet, her hands pressed together in front of her like she was praying, as if she were completely oblivious to what her hair was doing. She was walking towards the bed.

Her hair... the ponytail that grew from the back of her skull defied all sense, sliding along the ground behind her like a sidewinder, then winding around the bath tub, leading into it and then straight out again, taut to Clem's ankle where it was twisted so tight the skin was bleeding.

Clem crashed into the tub and cried out fit to wake the dead, then found himself back in the water briefly, his eyes and mouth full of soapy water before the hair yanked him out and dragged him around and around the tub and then towards the bed. He'd pulled half the heavy rug away from the floor, and got a glimpse of weird symbols carved into the boards before suddenly him found himself hanging upside down like a side of beef in a meat locker. Then he was flung face down on the bed with a jerk. He felt his right leg pop out of his hip joint and for a moment pain was his whole world. He roared into the sheets.

"Please, honoured guest," said Fuk Yu behind him, "Keep your voice. We have all night for screaming."

Clem groaned and flopped over on the bed.

"Jus' you c'mere," he spat, "Y'jus' come over here and I'll show you how t'fuckin' scream y'lil' *cunt.*"

Fuk Yu stood at the foot of the bed, her ponytail defying gravity as it turned in slow corkscrew loops above her head, a nightmare tornado, and some insane halo.

Then it struck, darting down like a snake.

Clem yelped and shut his eyes.

He felt the hair wrapping around both his wrists, and then both his ankles in figure eight loops. In another moment his arms were yanked up, his legs whipped up, his right leg screeching with pain, and he felt more loops coiling around and around binding his hands and feet together.

I've been hog tied, he thought, the idea so simple and so strange it couldn't be, and yet he knew that it was, *I've been trussed up like a hog 'bout to get its throat slit.*

He struggled a little, but then just relaxed. All of a sudden all the fight went out of him, as if his gut knew it was pointless to try and told his muscles to just give up. Something about being naked and tied up like an animal knocked the wind out of him and so he just stared up, looking at the ponytail hanging in the air.

"And now, we can begin," said Fuk Yu, and that was when Clem felt her toenails scrape at the stained pucker of his anus.

Clem thought, what *in the Hell is...* and then one cold, warped toe popped inside him and he stopped thinking anything at all.

"Ahh, so dry!" said Fuk Yu, "You need to relax, honoured guest, or this will be more pain than pleasure."

The toe popped out.

At the same time Clem farted.

A squeaker, but it was ripe.

The celestial sniffed the air. She smelled filth, delicious filth. The warm water on his guts had done its work.

Still balancing on one leg as gracefully as a crane, she pushed her foot up against Clem's anus again. His belly was already being squeezed by how he was being held up and this time when she pushed her toe into him she got the reaction she needed. Like a dam breaching, Clem's bowels opened up and hot, wet shit spurted out of him.

Fuk Yu let it flow over her foot, twirling her ankle to get her fist sized appendage evenly coated, rotten yellow faeces splattering onto the bedsheets.

Clem groaned into the bedsheets in the pure pleasure of release... but it was when Fuk Yu slid her foot up his ass right past the ankle that he came for the first time, the suddenly blood-solid tusk of his cock blasting gobs of salty fuck hard up over his own chest.

He had never felt anything like it. First there was the relief of shitting his guts out, and then suddenly his rectum was being stuffed full again, fuller, being filled past capacity; he felt his anus split and the ripping pain was another form of relief, all mixed together with the orgasm of having his prostate bumped with a toe.

Then he spoke. He didn't know he was about to speak, because he wasn't really thinking with any civilized part of his brain anymore. It was only one word, but it was the only word that Clem Tumblety would need until the very end of his Earthly existence;

"More."

Fuk Yu was a sculpture, perfectly balanced on one tiny, almost hoof like foot, with her other stuck up Clem's ass, her possessed ponytail curved over her back like a scorpion's tail, keeping the hog tied pelt trader suspended on what would have been the stinger.

"More?" she said, "Whatever honoured guest requests."

She eased her foot in further, pushing her toes deeper into him, greasy shit lubricating her slim shin as it entered.

Clem gasped and shuddered.

Oh gawd he wanted it all, he wanted to be filled up, filled up, stuffed...

"More..." he moaned.

Fuk Yu nodded in compliance, and withdrew her foot a little. But before Clem could protest she used the extra leverage to force forward even further, her shin disappearing up to the calf, and then beyond, up to her knee, cramming Clem's rectum to its fullest, her toes almost in his lower bowels.

Clem couldn't speak anymore. Instead he came again, shooting the last of his fuck in salty strings up and over his belly. He gasped raggedly.

Fuk Yu flexed her toes.

Clem's testicles twitched again, a last cough of cock snot jumping from the tip of his penis.

"...more..." he whispered.

Fuk Yu was stuck too deep to pull out for another thrust. Instead, she wound in her ponytail, pulling Clem onto her leg, skewering him.

She felt tough membranes and walls of muscle strain against her toes. The ponytail pulled back even harder... and those internal divisions burst.

Her foot speared up through the tangle of Clem's intestines in a hideous reverse hernia. His pelvis cracked as her thigh disappeared up his ass, his already ripped anus splitting all the way to his scrotum.

Fuk Yu felt the broad, smooth flank of his liver pass under the ball of her foot, and then his stomach squashed against the top.

Clem vomited, a fountain of bile and hard tack spraying from his lips.

Then her buckled toes pressed up against his heart... and her hair kept pulling him onto her leg... and his heart was pushed away from its mooring, further up into his chest... An aorta under strain tore, and that was how Clem Tumblety gained his citizenship in the Undiscovered Country.

Fuk Yu left him impaled and twitching on the length of her leg for a few minutes, letting the life flee, and then her ponytail pulled him off with a wet sucking noise, ending with a meat-pop as her foot finally emerged, followed by a flood of bloody and ripped tissue that splattered and puddled on the bed.

The ponytail laid the body on the ground almost delicately.

Then Hell began to feed not delicately.

KEVIN SWEENEY

CHAPTER I

His disciples came to him, saying, "Explain to us the parable of the weeds of the field." He answered them, "He who sows the good seed is the Son of Man, the field is the world; and the good seed, these are the children of the Kingdom; and the weeds are the children of the evil one. The enemy who sowed them is the devil."

Matthew 13:36–43

The albino rode into town on a donkey.

The creature was descended from the ass that had carried the Virgin to Bethlehem, and was the only creature that could approach such a damned place as it now plodded wearily into.

The albino was neither dying nor insane, and had no place in that town without a name. He had business but no place. He recognized the town for what it was, for why it had no name; names belonged to things which had known life, and this town had never been alive.

The town of Nowhere.

As he had journeyed in he had noted the things left behind. First were the bodies, horses for the main part, though sometimes mules, who had died and been left to rot only a day or twos ride from the town. Mostly they seemed to have died through exhaustion, or failed hearts, though with one or two there were signs of violence, their owners making the insane decision to kill the valuable beasts and continue towards Nowhere on foot.

Closer to the town, as he followed the tracks of men who now walked and those tracks only lead in one direction, he had spied bundles of possessions, the kinds of things folks needed for long journeys, sleeping rolls and sacks of provisions, just left; some were spilled out upon the dirt of the trail, as if they had been dropped as their owners walked, discarded carelessly. Others had been carefully hidden behind rocks and stunted brush, as if the owners planned to return for them but never had.

The albino knew what these things meant. The divestment of earthly goods. As if this were a spiritual pilgrimage.

The town was a U-shape, like a jawbone with the buildings as teeth. A saloon, a bank, a barbers, a general mercantile, a few houses in between them, ponderosa pine boards gleaming in the moonlight. They certainly looked like places of business and places where folks lived, but if you were to enter any of them you would step over the lintels of doorways onto dust, into rooms bare of even a stick of furniture. Motion pictures were years in the future, so one could not call it a set, could not use that as a reference point but that was all it was, a set, a reason for there being the one true place in town, a real tooth in a jaw set with hollow wooden ones.

The whorehouse. The *Half-World.*

The trail that lead to this town became the single street of the town that lead straight to the door of a three story parlour. It was a building as unremarkable as any of the others, with the sole difference that this one had life.

Sickly red light leaked from between pulled drapes.

In the dooryard was a fortune in coins and bills, scattered hither and yon, along with watches and rings and crucifixes and other discarded valuables. Not only the obvious items of value were found there, however, but objects that the albino recognized as closer to the hearts of men than even gold or silver; letters from loved ones long gone, mementos of childhood, spoils of war, souvenirs and scars picked up through a lifetime. Whatever was most valued was discarded at the threshold. That was the price of admission, but whatever was most valuable was the price taken inside.

The albino dismounted and hitched up the donkey.

He stood before the whorehouse, preparing himself spiritually for what was to come; he unzipped his pants and pulled out his immense snow-white penis, clasped his hands together in prayer around his cock, and muttered a rosary as he slowly masturbated.

"Hail Mary, full of *grace...*" was picturing the Blessed Virgin, belly swollen with childe…

The albino had pure white hair cut into a monk's *tonsure* and pink eyes that he shielded behind smoked spectacles. He was dressed like a gunfighter, an ankle length duster cloaking him. A dog's collar of black and white at his throat said he was a man of the cloth no matter what the holsters at his hips might suggest… though a closer inspection would show those holsters were not filled with guns.

THE WHOREHOUSE THAT JACK BUILT

He got through a dozen Hail Mary's before he came, blowing a cup of thick semen in fat gobs onto the coin scattered dirt of the dooryard.

He knelt and dipped two finger into the sticky fluid, then crossed himself.

Covered in spider-webs of his own spunk, the albino approached the door of the whorehouse... which opened to greet him spilling blood-light and screams of ecstasy.

*

The inside of the whorehouse was the size of a city.

In my father's house there are many mansions...

The door he entered was flanked by eunuchorns, creatures like minotaurs who had the heads of unicorns instead of bulls. As their name suggested, each of the massive beast-men had their horns snapped off and their genitals gouged out. Guards of the harem of Hell. It was they who had opened the door, and watched with hate-filled eyes as the albino strode without fear into…

The albino had once ridden through Monument Valley and the Half-World reminded him of that place of standing rock towers hundreds of feet tall only these towers were Babels given over to speaking the universal language of fucking and they stood not in a desert but a room the size of all the Earth.

The room he had stepped into was vast enough to contain buildings and yet was clearly still a parlour. The door he had stepped through was little more than a mouse hole, and he little more than a mouse, in a parlour whose floor was crowded with dozens of dolls houses... except they had no walls, were only the exposed insides of dolls houses, rooms open to view and in all of those rooms were being committed atrocities of love. In beds, on floors, against walls, straddling insane fuck-furniture, hung by hooks or chains or silk nooses, limbs entwining –legs, arms, tails, membranes, wings- teeth gnashing, biting, chewing, faces and cunts and anuses sucking and gushing and farting out weird fluids, gasps and moans and screams and croaking and laughter coloured through and through with madness.

The air was thick with unholy incense and the stench of sweat and semen, heavy enough to leave a sticky glaze of moisture on the albino's face.

"Welcome, pilgrim."

Over stimulated, the albino came to his senses to realize he was standing in one of those rooms without walls, a reception room filled with chaise lounges and love seats, all occupied by voluptuous demons of both genders, incubi and succubae, lascivious lamiae and perverse imps, rouged demon eyes

(the eyes of goats the goats go to the LEFT)

gazing at him as forked tongues played about lips and teeth. Hungry.

Scattered about the floor of the not-room were dolls houses, all of which were stripped of their walls. They seethed with movement, tiny doll movement. Microcosm and macrocosm. This room was a miniature of the greater room, and at the same time they were both the same room.

"As above, so below," said the voice that had welcomed him, a Scottish accent, "Aye, and around and around forever, forever, forever."

The voice was at his elbow. The albino looked down into a face he had memorised from the only known photograph taken of the subject. Marshall McGregor.

The architect of flesh.

The man was a dwarf and ugly as sin itself. Not only this, but obese and naked, his cock an enormous red horn that stood hard and proud from under rolls of hairy fat. The man was nearly as grotesque as some of the demon whore's who were his concubines.

Born to a wealthy laird in the highlands of Scotland, McGregor's soul was born as freakish as his body. A life of horrific excess funded by an early inheritance had laid the darkest of trails, a glistening slug trail that lead over a mountain of corpses, until finally he had made a deal with the devil-lord Arcimboldo.

"Many men of the church have stepped through mah door before now, pilgrim," said the dwarf, grinning, "So, I suppose it's a few bairns ye'll be wanting tae fuck? We've got a cherubim kept to one side for preachers and priests, though the poor wee thing is a bit ragged around the arse these days."

McGregor waddled to the middle of the parlour, holding his arms out as if to embrace his clutch of demonic whores.

"Or perhaps ye'd like to see a few more of me possibles first? Eh? Anything catch your eye? What's your poison, pilgrim? Cunt? Cock? Something a little more... exotic?"

The albino said nothing.

The demon whores began to lazily rise from where they lounged, each approaching the albino one by one. They slid and leered and danced around him, displaying what they had to offer; enormous breasts studded with dozens of bleeding nipples, forked cocks, cunts lined with eyeballs. Beast headed whores, whores with translucent jellyflesh, whores of rusted metal and rotten wood. A demon with a face like a smeared painting whispered filth in his left ear, another who's every head-hole was lined with white slug-bellies spoke sweetly in the other

The albino said nothing. The demons washed around him, an unmoving rock in a river of filth, foul waves washing over him.

McGregor was massaging the glans of his engorged penis, as big as a fist, sore and angry from overuse. An eyebrow crept up as the albino kept his peace.

"Now what's this? Cat got your tongue there pilgrim? Having second thoughts? Because if ye are, well, too fucking bad; the moment you stepped through the door the pact was sealed. One night of pleasure such as ye won't find this side of Paradise in exchange for every drop of blood, marrow, and semen in your body."

A bulb of pre-come the size of a walnut appeared at the tip of the dwarf's penis. He thumbed it up and into his mouth. He hummed in satisfaction before winking at the albino.

"And your soul, of course, but most folk who end up here have already forfeited that. So... what's your poison pilgrim? Make a choice or I'll choose for ye."

A drowned corpse with antlers of coral offered sea anemone orifices. A charred corpse, smoke still coiling from empty eyeholes and anus, croaked of charcoal pleasures. A rot bloated corpse promised a gash overflowing with pus and flesh-grubs.

The albino said nothing, but his impassive gaze finally slid away from the tempters to settle on the smirking dwarf.

"Satisfy me," said the albino.

McGregor stopped fondling himself.

"What'd ye say?"

The albino reached up with two fingers and pulled his smoked glasses further down his nose. His blood shot, pink eyes had no lines around them, making his age an impossible guess; did he not cry, did he not laugh?

"Satisfy me," he repeated.

The architect of flesh licked his fleshy lips and regarded the albino with narrowed eyes.

"Are ye challenging me, ye gobshite?"

The albino then expressed the first hint of any emotion. He grinned, fast, bright, no real emotion, just a token facial expression by a creature trying to communicate in another species' language.

"Just your whores. I've heard bold claims. I don't believe them."

"Ye what?"

"Your possibles..." the albino said, "Mediocre at best. My palm excites me more."

McGregor rubbed at his jaw and blinked rapidly, realizing that he was being insulted, that his right to this corner of Hell was being disputed, mocked. He stopped rubbing and waved a long, knuckly finger at the albino.

"Ye cheeky shite..." he muttered, rage building, "Ye cheeky fucking shite! Ye come into mah house and ye talk tae me like that? I'll fucking have your guts for garters ye cunt! I'll skin ye with mah own fucking teeth!"

The demon whores shrunk back from his anger, though it was not directed at them.

The albino's pink eyes gazed blandly over his smoked spectacles.

McGregor had threatened, but he had not moved. Of course not. A challenge had been issued, and he had no choice but to answer it. The supernatural world was constrained by laws as tightly as the world of men, just different laws. It was the reason *haints* could not enter a house unless invited... And why entering the Devil's house placed him entirely at your disposal, for as host he was bound to his guests every whim.

Marshall McGregor had made his pact and become a subject of such laws.

"I seek release," said the albino, "The standard bargain. My *corpus* for satiety. I doubt I'll get it, judging these."

McGregor ground his teeth.

"And if ye are unsatisfied by my whores? What stake do ye expect from me?" he asked slyly.

But the albino was slyer still. The grin returned.

"Nothing. Hell hates to forfeit. Hell will hold you accountable."

McGregor bared his teeth.

"Ye cunt," he spat.

"As you say."

McGregor rushed him, thundering forward on ponderous legs, his whole disgusting bulk in motion, his still erect cock bobbing. But he stopped short of actually touching the albino, his hands clutching at the air as if to rip him limb from limb.

The albino did not flinch.

Powerless, McGregor raged, every obscenity on his lips in a torrent of threats and promises and extravagant claims as to the albino's future.

That gentlemen took it all with bland indifference.

The occultist eventually ran out of puff and stood glaring up in raw hatred at the man whom he had extensive, gruesome destinies planned for.

"Ye cunt," he whispered.

The albino said;

"Satisfy me."

McGregor turned and stalked away. One of his whores didn't see the danger quick enough, and in a moment the heavy hipped creature with a sea horse head and tail was disembowelled. It was a reflex of anger, thrown away without thought.

No matter how comical his grotesque appearance, the dwarf was still one of the most dangerous humans on Earth.

The demon whores fell upon their sibling and ate her alive.

McGregor stomped on a dolls house and immediately, miles distant in the greater room, one of the massive buildings collapsed with a sound of thunder.

The albino was unmoved.

The architect of flesh finally reined in his passions enough to stop destroying things, and when he did inspiration struck him.

"Satisfaction is what ye seek, is it?" he asked, his back to the albino.

Above the sound of the whores eating, the albino said it was.

"And ye don't think any of my possibles here are gonnae do the trick, is that it?"

"Any of them? All of them? None of them."

McGregor turned around, and once more he was the courteous host.

"Sure, ye'd be a connoisseur of cunt then, and not just any pilgrim. Yes, ah see plain enough now! Ye will have to forgive me, its not like the sort of souls we're used to here have what ye'd call *refined pallettes*. No, no, none of these possibles is suited to a *connoisseur*. Ah find myself embarrassed!"

The albino had been warned of this line of reasoning. It was a loophole for a demonic host to wriggle out of responsbility.

"And seeing as though ah can't offer ye anything up to ye high standards, embarrasing as it might be, ah guess that means ye are..."

"I want the Vestals."

McGregor's act of gracious humility vanished in a moment.

"Ye what? The... how the fuck do ye..." the dwarf's eyes narrowed. The past decade of endless debauchery had addled his wits, so that only now it dawned on him to ask the question that mattered; "Who... *what* are ye?"

The albino's sickly eyes sparkled.

"Your questions," he said, " *Who, what,* don't matter. *Why*... I have been sent by the Sisters of the Immaculate to end what you began in Whitechapel."

THE WHOREHOUSE THAT JACK BUILT

The albino was normally a man of few words but he had prepared these for some long time as he tracked the occultist to the very edge of the frontier gleaning clues from whispered talk around campfires and hog ranches and missions until his final tip from a Pinkterton agent gutshot and dying in delerium had lead him here to the very edge of manifest blasphemy.

"I'm here for a sexorcism."

The albino's filthy poncho fell from about his shoulders to reveal that he was naked underneath except for a pair of spurs and holsters that held not guns. He was coyote-lean and moon-pale, his sinews a map of bite scars, his back furrowed by claws in ecstasy. A rosary of razorblades wrapped around his right wrist. Between his legs hung heavy his circumcised cock, a rope fist-knotted at the end; it was enormous, though more shocking still was the colors of it. Rainbow hued, from root to bell head, all seven shades from red through to violet.

McGregor had bound demons to his whim and now was bound himself by the lore of the land; he could not refuse the custom of any who crossed the threshold willing to trade. Even if they came asking for the rarest of pleasures, pleasures that he kept for himself, and even then only indulged lightly.

Forget the exaggerated sex between its thighs, this sickly looking creature wouldn't survive Mary, let alone the others.

McGregor grinned to himself. Then he began to laugh. His laughter grew from deep chuckling into great bales that rolled about the not-room. The demons who ate of their kind leered up with bloody mouths and joined the laughter, teeth claggy with smouldering flesh, screeching and hooting like beasts.

"Ye come here wantin' for the Vestals... a pasty wee ferret-faced fucker like ye? By Christ, the Sisters aren't what they were if they're havin' to recruit the likes of ye! Ye may be as big as a fuckin' donkey, but the Vestals..." the dwarf stopped laughing with a snap, "I'll have 'em save ye skull so's I can shit in it."

If the albino took note of the threat he showed nothing, just gripped his cock with both hands and began to work his inches, impatient. He swiftly began to stiffen, to swell.

"Fancy talk's finished. Where're the whores?"

The dwarf's face turned red, then beetroot; his mouth opened and closed like a fish, unable to find any way to express what seethed within him.

And then his color cleared. His eyes darkened.

"Alreet," he said, and clapped his hands, twice.

In a moment everything was different, as if they were in a theatrical production and a scenery change had been called; the skeleton architecture of the room and the Hell-Whores themselves were whipped away up into the darkness until the albino and the dwarf stood alone and exposed surrounded by doll houses on the floor of the vaster room filled with mansions.

The dwarf stooped and picked up one of the dolls houses and the albino recognised it as a replica of the outside of the Half-World.

"D'ye want a wee peek at what's tah come?" asked McGregor with a sneer. He lifted the roof of doll whorehouse and tilted it towards the albino, who caught a glimpse of five miniature rooms; one was a squalid garret, another inside of a redskin's teepee, and yet another was the inside of a backwoods shack, filled with bizarre taxidermy. But what were the last two rooms? The glimpse gave only impressions, one of an Egyptian tomb, and the other a cave with crude paintings on the walls...

The dwarf snapped the lid down and dropped the model building on the ground at his feet and at once an entire building dropped silent from the darkness above to land behind him. The effect was disconcerting indeed, as if an elephant had plummeted to Earth only to land as softly as a feather. More disconcerting still was the fact that it was the building they were already in, the Half-World.

(as above so below)

McGregor grinned.

"Ye ever seen those Russian dolls preacher? Little wooden things they are, one nesting snug inside the other, and another inside that, and another inside that, and on and on."

The door to the Half-World opened. No light spilled out, but shadow did, as if it had substance.

The dwarf's eyes never left the albino who was striding past him, titanic rainbow hued cock swinging.

"Five vestals, preacher," said McGregor, "That's what ye asked for, and that's what ye'll get. For yer flesh, for yer blood, fer yer seed and yer soul. And when they've finished with ye..." the albino paid no notice, disregarding the dwarf, who became incensed, "Wha', hoy, ye divn't DARE ignore ME ye cunt! HOY! *Ye cheeky gobshite, ah'll fuckin'...*"

The albino was already at the threshold. How many Hell-Whorehouses had he sexorcised? How many of their owners had made tedious speeches about how they were going to defecate in his hollowed skull, and wipe their rectums with the ragged remains of his soul?

Not slowing, without ego and so without fear, he stepped into the darkness as the dwarf raged behind him in the vastness of the outer room;

"AH'LL HAVE YER FUCKIN' GUTS FER GARTERS YE CUNT! D'YE FUCKIN' HEAR ME? AH'LL..."

The door closed and the silence of the darkness was deafening.

*

Within the house was a ruin of a parlour room, cold, dark. The roof was long collapsed to expose a sky full of constellations never seen upon Earth. The door he had passed through was one of six that lead into and out of the room.

The parlour was the kind of room in which gentlemen would pass the time waiting for their favorite soiled dove to become available, reading, smoking, or dreaming of what was to come.

This ruined room was strewn with broken furniture, scattered books. Upon one wall hung a sampler in a shattered frame. Whores had to pass the time too. Needlework kept clever hands clever.

The albino gazed around the room, and saw each door had a name burned upon it, or scrawled in chalk, fingered in blood, carved with a bone knife…

Mary Maggie Darling.
Bear-Maiden.

THE WHOREHOUSE THAT JACK BUILT

Grandma Spuckler.

Clitocris.

Ginger.

The albino's gaze settled once more upon the sampler hanging crooked upon a wall of rain warped boards. His eyes favored the pale glow of the alien constellations, adjusted easier to it then to candles and gas, and by weird starlight the albino read this message picked out in stitches:

The PARABLE of the LOCK & the KEY

The LOCK that can be opened with many keys is a Very Bad Lock.

But the KEY that opens many locks is a Very Good Key.

A key turned. A lock opened. A door began to open and within it was darkness into which the albino walked naked.

CHAPTER II

"And I will put enmity between thee and the woman, and between thy seed and her seed; it shall bruise thy head, and thou shalt bruise his heel."

Genesis 3:15

(In the Garden how many were there that went on two legs there were three that went on two legs Adam and Eve and the Other)

(Who is the Son of God He is His own Son)

The Motherfucker Superior drank Holy Water until her stomach bulged below her bare tits, tits as sagging and wrinkled as old eggplants, long nipples pointing at the ground.

"In the Talmud," she croaked, gasping from having drunk so much, "It is written that demons outnumber humans by millions, are responsible for all illness and disease, and yet remain invisible to the eye of man."

He knelt before the font, finger shuffling bead by bead through a rosary as he recited prayers.

The Motherfucker Superior smiled down at him, a smile of thin-worm lips rimmed with downy fur. A hundred years old, her every inch of flesh showed it, from the infinite complexity of wrinkles that sagged her face to the stretch marks and liver spots and loose knit cheesy skin that hung in folds from her bony carcass of a body.

"Some years ago men of science, bacteriologists they were called, found staphylococci, streptococci, coli bacilli, Loeffler's bacillus, and other bacteria in samples of Holy Water taken from this very church. But it was only sanctified, not purified."

He never slowed a moment from his prayers as the Motherfucker Superior caressed the mottled skin of her bloated belly with one hand, as if her decayed womb had at last fulfilled a destiny her calling had denied, as if it were heavy with child and not sanctified water. Her other hand held the aspergillum, a perforated metal ball on the end of a wooden handle that was used during Mass to sprinkle the Holy Water about.

"The germ theory of disease states that organisms so small as to be invisible to the human eye are responsible for sickness and ill-health. Once again, we find the sciences only just beginning to understand what religion already knew."

She shoved the aspergillum up her cunt and started to masturbate with it.

Prayer still fell from his lips as he thumbed each bead of the rosary through his left fist, his right hand steadily working his foreskin back and forth. His balls were still in agony from the branding, but he did not falter as he flogged his meatus.

They soon fell into a rhythm, matching each other stroke for stroke, like pistons in a steam engine perfectly engineered.

Between moans, Motherfucker Superior continued with the lesson;

"Holy Water... can cast out demons... but only... when it has been purified first..."

The mutual masturbation pitched, peaked, reached a crescendo as a dual round of shouting in tongues as he shot his seed across the baptismal font and the Motherfucker Superior found release as well.

Such release as loosened her bladder.

Pissing onto his face, effusion by urination into his open eyes, his upturned mouth gulping the golden goodness flushed clean by her kidneys, she concluded the lesson with Acts 2:17;

"'And in the last days I will pour out my spirit upon every sort of flesh, and your sons and your daughters will prophesy and your young men will see visions and your old men will dream dreams.'"

And he saw a vision his eyes washed with her divine salty piss cleared and he saw many mansions he SAW...

*

All women bleed once a month, though most not so from their palms.

The albino sexorcist knew it all started with this one. It was with this fallen woman that McGregor made the pact that resulted in the murders of five other prostitutes, and the horrors that came after.

She didn't look like much. Mary Maggie Darling was no more remarkable than any other Cockney flower girl deflowered and forced to take cock on her knees.

Except, of course, for the wounds.

THE WHOREHOUSE THAT JACK BUILT

The first of the five Vestal Whores lay on a filthy mattress with her legs spread wide to expose the rose of her sex. She was drinking from a bottle of wine, guzzling whenever she wasn't speaking.

"'Ello, flower," she said, her East End accent twisting *flower* into *flahh,* "So, the boss says you reckon you're gonna gimme a bloody good seein' too? Well, we'll see, alrigh', we'll fackin' see!"

The room was a hovel painted a butchershop nightmare. The center of the chaos was the bed where the whore lay, a horse-hair mattress soaked through and through with blood from which radiated a demented pattern of bloody handprints across every wall, as if a blind slaughterman had sought an exit.

Darling wore but a whalebone girdle, fingerless gloves, and a grin full of rotten teeth, her hair a greasy black nest, a fake beauty spot on her upper lip and her right pupil permanently dilated. She spotted the albino's cock, gestured with her bottle of wine.

"An' what's this then? Well, looks like the lad's at least got a peggo for the job! Lemme just get wet for you, love, need to be nice 'n' slippy to get that hog's leg up me snatch!"

Saying this, she stuck the neck of the wine bottle up her cunt and pumped it back and forth.

"Unnnnhhh! Yerrr! 'Ere we go!"

Darling suddenly pulled the bottle neck out of herself with a wet pop and threw it against the far wall with a smash; as if she had removed a bung the whore pissed herself, a rope of bright yellow leaping out between her legs to splash the already blood soaked sheets she lay on. She cackled as the stream puddled and overflowed the bed, a thunderous rush of vinegar-urine so steaming-strong that it stung the albino's sensitive eyes even though he stood yards from the bed.

He felt the tears flow down his cheeks. It made him nostalgic for a second; it had been a long time since he had cried from any kind of emotion.

Darling kicked her heels in glee, splashing piss every which way.

"Climb aboard!" she crowed, "Come and plug me up if ya can!"

The albino pulled at his cock and walked towards the laughing whore, his bare feet sticking and unsticking from boards painted with drying blood and then stepping into the growing pool of urine that waterfalled from the bed.

Hail Mary full of grace... radiant with her pregnancy...

Each of the Vestal whores was a flesh and blood perversion of one of the Nazarene's miracles. Like in a Black Mass where the altar was replaced with the body of a prostitute and the Host was the blood and flesh of infants, so each of the Vestals was a mockery of one of the testaments of Jesus's ministry.

Turning water into wine...

Wine into urine.

By the time he reached the foot of the bed and knelt one knee onto the sopping mattress he was at full mast, his swollen purple glans as fat as a giant plum, and the whore had stopped laughing as she gazed along the vein-straining length of him.

"Well, well," she said, smirking as he crawled up between her thighs, "'Oo's a big boy then?"

She grunted, straining; an extra hard stream of piss shot up his belly and chest. She burst out cackling again, clearly insane.

"Put a cork in it," said the albino, gripping her bony hips, and so saying he stuffed the fat fist of his glans into her and shoved the first seven inches in. The piss stream stopped as her stretched full cunt pinched her urethra shut.

"Uggghhhnnn," Darling gasped, then laughed, "Oh fack me, treacle! Fack me!"

He pulled back, rammed her again, pulled back, rammed, each time being squirted with piss.

Then he stopped.

"Ugggh... Hmmm? Izzat it?" she leered up into his face, her crazy eyes dancing, "Crook it in twice and squirt dearie? Eh? *Faugh!* Should've known it was all for show!"

The albino said nothing. The stench of her decaying teeth and sour wine was making it difficult to set himself to the task of destroying her cunt, but what was worse was he couldn't get a good grip, every surface of skin slippery with piss.

Darling squirmed under him, squeezing and rubbing herself up and down the length of fat cock inside her.

"C'mon ya snifflin' shit," she growled, "Blow yer load and give up! Yer damned and ya know it, so shoot yer fuck already!"

The albino took hold of the laces that bound her corset, finally securing a proper grip.

"Better," he muttered, and then he really started to fuck her, pulling out and finally slamming the whole thirteen inches of himself up into her cunt so hard he smashed her head against the blood-crusty wall. His grip secure he pounded her back and forth, turning her into a rag doll unable to resist.

The whore squawked and howled, taken surprise by the sudden ferocity of the attack as the colossal cock split her. As used as she was to being violated with bottles, cudgels, fists, the albino's immense column of engorged flesh was something else entirely. It was HUGE and it had a PULSE, a throb louder than her own heart had ever been, when there had still been a heart to beat within her.

Flesh on flesh he SAW...

She was seven years old an orphan taken in by the sisters of Our Lady of Sorrow now due to make her First Holy Communion and Father Finuncane took a special interest in getting her ready for it he insisted on giving her a Very Private lesson in how she should receive the Host into her mouth he had made her kneel down and close her eyes and open her mouth and then something that smelled bad and tasted meaty was in her mouth and Father Finuncane told her he was going to give her communion wine and her mouth had flooded with hot salty musty tasting fluid she had swallowed as much as she could but it overflowed her mouth and she was so afraid of the Sacred wine spilling upon the ground that she had used her hands as a bowl to catch it but when it touched her palms they blossomed into ragged wounds through which the golden stream poured.

Father Finuncane made her promise to keep the miracle a secret until he could confirm the matter with his brother priests and it wasn't long before she found herself showing many many many more priests how she took communion and the wonderful thing that happened to her when their piss spilled from her mouth into her hands and after that the church bought her and she entered the ranks of the Little Children who Suffered.

She grew up but unlike so many of the other Little Children she was not murdered when she grew old beyond the tastes of priests on account of her gift but a young adult is stronger and craftier than a child and when she saw her chance she escaped and found herself living upon the streets of London but all the gin she could swallow for which she exchanged every coin she made upon her back could not get the taste of piss out of her mouth and she kept her stigmata a secret but secrets get out and one night she was approached by a man who was interested only in those holes in her hands rather than between her legs and he was certainly no priest no he was a different kind of monster who was heading to the New World and that she would be joining him...

And so Mary Maggie Darling became the acolyte of the dwarf, who helped him select his victims, to lure them, to keep a lookout whilst he conducted the rites that lead them out of this life and he cut out their cunts and they became the Gashes he would later use...

The pain and sadness of her years as worthless street meat, her conversion by the architect and her elevation to a Vestal of the *Half-World*, to glorious insanity and endless horror... all were forgotten by a sensation she had only a trace memory of ever having had before. Beyond the pain of her cervix being smashed, beyond the pain of her pussy being stretched so wide it felt old wounds might bloom, healed vaginal tears from who knew how many savage rapes ready to split wide again... there was joy.

It felt like the promise of dawn, the hint of light on the horizon of darkness.

The albino was muttering in her ear.

"...thy kingdom *come*, thy will be *done*..."

Mary Maggie Darling didn't know what a sexorcism was, but suddenly something savaged screwed itself more firmly into her spirit, the worm of corruption that had made her rotten soul its home, recognising the joy for what danger it posed.

Her eyes darkened, both good and blown pupils suddenly swallowed by a maelstrom of black. Her hands gripped the albino's buttocks, dug cracked and split fingernails into his flesh.

"*Wrong hole preacher!*" she snarled, and began to buck back against him.

Wrong hole.

Shit.

The albino stopped thrusting and tried to push himself away from her, knowing how close to losing everything he was. Her ruined nails carved burrows in his buttocks and back, clinging onto him even as her hips continued to grind against him, as the walls of her worn pussy clamped his cock and tried to prevent his inches sliding out before he came.

He pulled slowly, getting almost half of himself out before he felt the dangerous twitching in the tip that said he was about to blow.

The albino loosed one hand from the laces of her corset and punched the whore in the face.

She spat out two teeth, and she laughed.

"*Yearr, preacher, thassit! Knock me fackin' teeth out, show me you care!*"

The albino made as if to swing again but did not, instead suddenly pitching himself sideways, throwing his whole body weight to one side with his feinted punch. Caught off guard and her grip as slippery with piss as his had been, Darling lost her handholds on his flesh and that was enough; the last half foot of his penis slid free of her cunt with a wet sucking.

The albino hit the floor and felt himself come, his balls contracting and spasming as ivory fuck shot in gluey strings out of his massive cock across the whore's thigh.

They splattered, sizzled, *burned.*

Darling screeched as the clammy skin of her leg began to smoke, as if the semen were acidic.

The albino groaned, cupping his testicles.

The voice of the Motherfucker Superior was in his head:

We take the word TESTIFY from the Latin word TESTES. In Roman court a man swore not on a Bible as now, but cupped that which was most precious to him.

"What the fack izzis?!" howled Darling, hands hovering over her thigh but not daring to touch the hissing fluid that bubbled there, "What the fack is wrong with yer muck?!"

The albino lying on the ground gripped his still firm cock in one hand and lifted it clear of his testicles to show the branding; his scrotum was scarred with a burnt-in icthysis, the fish symbol of the early Church.

His balls were blessed. His every ejaculation was Kingdom Come.

She snarled.

"Yearr, well it don't matter no-how," she said, glancing at her peeling, blistered skin, "When a man drops 'is muck thassit, 'e's all in. So why don't you be a good boy..." one gloved hand had slid beneath the filthy pillow under her head, "and just fackin' die now?"

She pulled out a straight razor and sat up on the bed.

The albino shook his head, and cock in fist wagged the maggot end at her.

Hail Mary FULL of grace...

"Ain't satisfied," he told her, stiffening.

Unsteady after the assault on her vault and the bubble-burnt flesh of her thigh, Mary Maggie Darling tottered up from the bed just as the albino scooted back and clambered to his heels.

Urine streamed down her leg, washing away the last of his clinging, burning semen. Her corset was half untied and sagging on one side, her hair in rat tails around her face, her blown pupil glaring out from amidst a greasy black skein.

"I'm goin' to peel yer fackin' face and wipe my arse with it," she spat, razor blade snatching back and forth in the air.

(heard that one a few times before)

The albino stood naked before her, peggo already hard and ready to go again, gunless holsters at his hips and spurs on his ankles.

Wrong hole... but he had an idea which was the right one...

He held his arms out wide, a cross, a temptation. A mockery of her affliction.

Darling screeched and lunged, more fury than skill. The albino stepped back twice, missing one, two swings of the blade, and on the third grabbed her wrist and pulled her to him, turning his hip into her belly and flipping her over it like a greased ball bearing.

She did a full flip and slammed face first onto the crusted floorboards, her collarbone snapping, the razor dashing away. The wind knocked from her, Darling could only gasp.

The albino was on her in a moment, slamming one knee into the small of her back and rabbit punching her kidneys as hard as he could.

"Piss blood, whore," he told her, grabbing her gloved hands and pulling them behind her.

Wrong hole...

He gripped her wrists in one large hand and stripped the fingerless gloves with his other to reveal the weeping, bloody wounds in her palms, as if rude nails had been pounded through them.

Stigmata. The wounds of the Nazarene manifest.

This was why the architect had begun the ritual with this otherwise faceless whore. Somehow her tainted flesh was a conduit to the mystery, rending itself in sympathetic agony to the crucified man of sorrows.

"Gerroff me ya fackin' bastard!" screeched Darling, finding her voice again and struggling, "Gerrof me, gerroff..."

The albino jerked her arms up tighter, nearly pulling them from their sockets and drove his knee harder into her spine.

Her hands were crossed one over the other, the wounds lined up.

The Motherfucker Superior's words, one of the catechisms, the parables, the endless lessons driven into his skull at the seminary;

It is easier for a camel to pass through the eye of a needle...

He rammed his cock into the double hole of the stigmata, shoving half a foot of muscle straight through the palms of her hands. The long bones of her fingers were splayed wide at his passing, his girth pushing them apart.

"What the fack..." Darling croaked.

The albino knelt more fully on her, a knee pressed into each kidney, and forced her to give him the ultimate handjob, sawing his whole thirteen inches back and forth, fucking the bones and tendons lubricated with the blood that was spackled in prints across the walls.

He pictured the Blessed Mother in his mind, heavy with Childe, and wrapped his hands around the other half of his cock, sticking through the other side of the whore's hands.

Hail Mary full of...

"GERROFF ME!"

Darling's violent outburst, a roared demand and a massive spasm of her muscles, caught the albino off-guard. Like an untamed mustang she heaved and thrashed under him.

He had nothing to support himself and found himself pitched backward. He was still gripping his cock, and as his whole weight was thrown his mammoth rope of blood and veins ripped the whore's hands in half, splitting up between the middle and ring fingers.

She screeched as the albino's shoulders hit the filthy floor, knocking the breath from him and bouncing the back of his skull off the boards. He lay where he was a moment, stunned, hips still jerking rhythmically.

"Me 'ands! Me fackin' 'ands, what've you done to me fackin' 'ands!"

The albino raised his head a little, dazed.

The whore had turned over and sat up, her corset almost hanging off her, her legs wide to displaying her angry cunt. She was staring at him through the ruins of her stigmata, bloody white roots that leaned at impossible angles to one another. She looked like a ruined china doll.

Then she started to heal.

As the albino watched, the long bones of her hand folded back together, like a collapsed fan being closed up, and the split skin began to knit an insect-busy seething of tissue.

Erectoplasm, said a memory, a theoretical lesson at the seminary on the biology of Hell, *According to a belief of the Hindoo's, it takes thirty drops of blood, to make a drop of bone marrow, and thirty drops of marrow to make a single drop of semen. And if "the blood is the life..."*

All the damned were formed of the same primal jelly. It was why the *Half-World* was in business, the collection of the raw material.

Darling's hands had healed, save for the weeping stigmata.

"Still got the wrong 'oles, preacher," she spat, and picked up the straight razor from where it had fallen.

The albino clambered to his feet almost as the whore found hers, barely upright swift enough to dodge the next swing of the blade, Darling's face a wild grin of crusted teeth and domino eyes.

She grunted with each swing, the blade whickering the damp air, and the albino felt the wind on his lips as he snapped his neck back only barely.

He fell back upon the piss drenched bed, his calves knocked from under him.

Darling howled and whipped the razor over her razor, aiming for his balls.

The blade cleaved into his thigh, narrowly missing the fleshy eggs aimed at.

Hissing at the bite of steel, the albino swung his legs wildly like an animal on its back; his right heel clipped the whores waist.

Darling squawked, her eyes widening, then with a groan pitched onto the bed next to him.

She lay face down in the urine, moaning.

"Uhhhhnnnn... *cunt...*"

The albino lay next to her breathing hard, puzzled. The sound she was making was familiar. All men knew it, and rarely discovered that women could know it too. But it made no sense; he had felt the heel of his foot hit her in the side of her waist, felt the whalebone in her corset crack. The moaning of the whore was that of a creature struck below the waist, between the legs.

He looked down at his thigh; saw the first inch of the razor dug into his flesh. Wincing, he pulled it free and flung it far across the room.

When he was once more stood, beside the bed, the whore had rolled herself over and was hugging her side.

Wondering, he reached down and pulled her fingers away. She batted at his hand.

"Nooo..."

Before she could stop him he ripped her corset off.

Wrong 'ole.

Still got the wrong 'oles, preacher.

In the side where he had kicked her was a vagina.

Stigmata; holes in the hands and feet, as if nailed to a cross, crucified... but the fifth wound was a hole in the side where a Roman centurion had speared the dying Nazarene "and blood and water flowed forth."

But this wound had labia.

He heard the dwarf, one of her memories in his own mind.

Hell needs fuel, lassie. The internal-infernal *combustion engines require flesh and fluids in the way that locomotives require coke and coal. But nothing of the unseen world is simple, and special rituals are required to funnel blood and marrow and seed to the engines. Cunts are needed. They are the very gates of life, and as all infernal Lores ran on perversions of the sacred, so the gates of the ultimate mystery are ruined and made ugly. The cunt of a whore, brutally murdered, becomes a Gash in the membrane of the material plane through which God's children may willingly throw away the gifts He has given them. And Hell, in turn, can birth its children through those upon whom God had wasted a soul...*

A Whitechapel whore had been vivisected and her sex thaumaturgically attached to Darling's flesh. This was where the first stolen cunt had been hidden, the first keyhole he had to break.

The albino mounted the bed, his cock hard and righteous, balls swollen with blessed spunk.

Mary Maggie Darling sensed the danger and tried to roll away.

"No ya don't preacher, yer'll not..."

He punched her in the throat to shut her up. She squawked and smacked at him, drove a knee up to catch his jaw, but each blow he knocked back with his free hand, his other holding her down. She was weak from their tussling so far, from her body having to repair itself. She grabbed at his balls and he backhanded her; she clawed at his belly and he backhanded her; soon she not more than twitched before his fist smashed into her mouth, hitting her over and over, until she was still long enough for him to lash her wrists to the bedstead with his rosary.

"No!" she croaked, goat eyes burning from the bloody mess of her face, thrashing her legs and jerking about as much as she could, "No no no no no..."

She continued to buck until he stuck his cock into the cunt yawning beside her abdominal muscles. As pre-come dribbled from the end he squeezed his bloated tip in, felt dark energies crackling like static electricity in the walls of the vagina. Of course these alien sexes lead not into a place of birth, but instead his vein riddled meatus slid between muscle and into the warmth of the whore's bowels, into the twisted ropes of her intestines.

She shuddered, perhaps from pain, and then Darling laughed, defeated and... Grateful?

"Go on then preacher; finish this," she croaked, "Up to yer nuts in guts."

His pink eyes studied her face.

"Do you want the last rites?" he asked.

Her head rolled back and forth weakly.

"This is just a carcass, preacher. Me soul is down below, beyond the reach of yer prayers. Finish this preacher; fuck me."

He began to pump, to thrust, to pound, long, slow strokes of his entire length, slamming himself into her right up to his pelvis, his balls slapping her side. Her belly would swell with each lunge, distended by the huge cock being crammed into the already packed space of her abdominal cavity.

It was like fucking a sack of skinned snakes, skinned snakes that had been rotting, their flesh slimy with decay. The whore took it, breathing shallow, gulping occasionally as if she had eaten a meal too fast and it was playing up on her.

Watching his cock seething under her flesh helped the albino to focus, even as Darling belched, her breath smelling of bile and flesh.

The albino sped up, sliding in and out and grinding his hips and muttering the Lord 's Prayer over and over, keeping pace with the flow of the words.

"...thy Kingdom COME... they will be DONE..."

Darling belched again.

"Oh fack," she moaned, her lips speckled with greasy fragments.

The albino barely noticed, losing himself in the moment, chasing after the orgasm which would finish this, break the first of the keyholes and bring him one step closer to completing his divinely appointed mission. One of the gates of life and death stood ajar and he must close it.

The motion of his immense organ working through the whore's intestines was forcing half-digested material to work backwards, the wrong way. Some previous meal flesh of a past patron was being squeezed upwards; it was this that was making her burp.

The albino strokes were frantic now as he rapidly recited the prayer of exorcism;

"Lorem ipsum dolor sit amet," pounding and pounding, *"Consectetur adipisicing elit, sed do eiusmod tempor incididunt ut labore et dolore magna aliqua,"* thrusting and thrusting and thrusting, *"Ut enim ad minim veniam, quis nostrud exercitation ullamco laboris nisi ut aliquip ex ea commodo consequat,"* like the buildup of electricity in the air before a lightning strike, *"Duis aute irure dolor in reprehenderit in voluptate velit esse cillum dolore eu fugiat nulla pariatur,"* come boiling spilling over into his shaft tightening ready to blow *"Excepteur sint occaecat cupidatat non proident, sunt in culpa qui OFFICIA deserunt MOLLIT anim ID EST LABORUM... AMEN!"*

He ejaculated hard, smashing his entire length into her as deep as he could go, pumping blast after blast of semen into the bolus of her intestines.

THE WHOREHOUSE THAT JACK BUILT

Almost simultaneously, the force of his assault became too much for Darling's digestive organs, half-digested meat forced from her intestines back up into her stomach which revolted one final time, causing the whore to belch again, only this time she did not stop but followed through, the burp becoming a rushing stream of vomit dredged from her rancid guts that thundered down her own chest and belly.

The fire in her goat eyes winked out, her life snuffed in a moment.

His immense cock still twitching even as the glow of orgasm began to fade, the albino regarded the wash of vomit as an omen. Amidst the stringy connective tissue and glistening cobs of fat he saw teeth and knots of hair, the various scraps that the demon whores fed on, he seemed to read the future as some men will in a handful of tossed bones upon the desert floor.

He pulled his cock out of the whore's bowels, the sight of his entire length wet with blood almost like her cooling intestine slithering free, noticing that the vagina rudely stitched into her side was withered now, desiccated, completely unable to bear life. The lock was broken. This gate would not open again.

He used two fingers to close the whore's eyes, made the sign of the cross on her forehead, and stood up from the bed.

His cock was still hard, a barber's pole of spunk and blood.

"Requiem in pace, bitch," he muttered.

CHAPTER III

"Ye are of your father the devil, and the lusts of your father ye will do."

John 8:44

(In the Garden how many were there that went on two legs there were three that went on two legs Adam and Eve and the Other.

(Who is the Son of God He is His own Son.

(What was its name that was the Other the Other in the garden was called the Serpent.

(Who was the mother of God the Virgin Mary was the mother of God.)

The Motherfucker Superior crammed another flamingo brain into her mouth and continued to speak, spraying clods of snotty tissue;

"During the miracle of transubstantiation ordinary bread and wine become the flesh and blood of the Redeemer. He is often referred to in medieval literature as a pelican. Saint Thomas Aquinas writes in Adoro te devote; Lord Jesus, Good Pelican, wash me clean with your blood, one drop of which can free the entire *world of all its sins. Even Dante refers to Him as 'mankind's pelican'."*

A Roman feast; the church had been born of Rome, and retained tattered vestments of the Empire. An extravagant beano fit for the table of a Cesar was spread before the Motherfucker Superior. The Romans cared more for extravagance than taste, and the table reflected that in its theme of Cloud Cuckoo Land. Roasted and fried and stuffed larks, peacock, swans, swallows, parrots... and she ate of all of them, cramming greasy handfuls into her mouth, uncaring whether she stripped leg meat with her teeth or crunched through beaks and eyes, insatiable in appetite as she spoke.

"In some medieval bestiaries the pelican is said to kill its young with love; it caresses them with its talons and rips them apart. Sometimes its young are said to be killed by a Serpent. In grief the bird rips open its own breast with its beak and feeds the corpses with its own blood, and brings them once again to life. The parallels of symbolism between the bird and the Redeemer are obvious."

The albino was at her side. He had no chair, but crouched upon the floor with no food.

"The communion host of bread and wine is placed upon the tongue with a benediction. The way most birds feed their young is well known."

She paused from her devouring to produce a long feather. She opened her mouth and angled the feather in, tilting her head back to accommodate its length, until the fine edge tickled her oesophagus just right and she turned to the albino and vomited into his open, upturned mouth.

KEVIN SWEENEY

He ate. The quantity overflowed his mouth, splattered down his cheeks and chin, but he guzzled what he could, gulping down half chewed chunks, clotted knots of cartilage and popped muscle dripping with saliva and stomach acid.

When she had little left to give and the albino had trouble swallowing anymore the Motherfucker Superior wiped her mouth and set herself to pray, quoting from the testament;

"What goes into a man's mouth does not make him unclean, but what comes out of his mouth, that is what makes him unclean."

And then she ate again.

*

The cannibal was eating every flesh except human.

The room was a huge Injun wigwam, smoke-murky, dream-catchers of scalp hair hung from the obscured ceiling and totem poles of those scalped heads, each with its genitals stuffed in its mouth, rose behind the horror he had to fuck.

Bear-Maiden was an obese Injun whore, a naked, sweating expanse of redskin flesh nearly as huge as a covered wagon. She sat cross legged on woven blanket, her thighs each as huge as a foals belly supporting a vast gut draped in rolls of fat, upon which her enormous breasts lolled. Atop all this was her head, tiny atop the enormous cheese wheels which were her chins, a face of high cheekbones and dark eyes, a face painted for war with black chevrons. She wore a necklace of severed ears that was so tight around her bloated throat it seemed to be throttling her.

THE WHOREHOUSE THAT JACK BUILT

The pile of animals the whore was devouring was almost as large as herself, a screeching, mewling mountain of still living creatures, limbs broken and then flung one atop the other within reach of her hands and mouth; the albino's brief glance showed raccoons, quail, porcupines, possums, rabbits, skunks, groundhogs and other critters, spines or necks snapped, making noises if they could, sides heaving.

She ate them alive.

The albino watched her pick up a bullfrog and ram the creature's head into her mouth, teeth filed to points that snapped down and with a twist of her neck beheaded it, barely chewing before she swallowed. She held the limp grey body aloft in one hand and squeezed its internal organs out into her mouth and gulped them down.

She stripped the flesh from its legs and discarded the rest into a glistening pile of bones and fur at her left side.

Her hand reached forth again and seized a squirrel. The creature was breathing rapidly and its eyes were glassy with panic, its head pinched between obese finger and thumb; with her free hand she twisted off its tail with a grisly rip, throwing the inedible bush into her scrap pile. Then the mountain of woman-flesh opened her mouth wide and fed the creature down between her teeth, like a mechanical thresher, chewing through the animal from its hind legs upwards, relishing the thin hot blood that sprayed her face as the critters panicked heart beat faster and faster.

That heart was the clapper in the bell of its ribcage, stopped when pointed teeth bit into it like a cherry.

"Hungry, hungry whore," muttered the albino.

She heard him. Dark eyes, goat eyes, gazed across the expanse of her body at him, ropes of bloody saliva drooling from the corners of her mouth and dripping down her chins. She threw the squirrels head away and grinned her cannibal grin, filed teeth claggy with flesh.

"Palest of pale faces," she said, her voice a rumble of prairie thunder, "Bear-Maiden has waited heap big long time. Bear-Maiden is empty. Come fill Bear-Maiden."

A slug-tongue oozed out of her mouth and ran around her lips.

"Or does palest face want Bear-Maiden to smoke-um his *peace pipe?*" she leered.

The albino had the rosary wrapped around his wrist and his holsters were on his naked hips, but all he truly needed was already rearing up righteous between his legs again, still eager to fuck the damned back to Hell.

Though reaching her cunt presented a problem; sweating rolls of redskin fat obscured her crotch.

Bear-Maiden laughed, making her whole body quiver.

The albino advanced, gripping himself around the base of his rainbow coloured cock with both hands; he pumped his shaft like he was chambering a round into a shotgun.

Bear-Maiden crammed a quail with broken legs into her mouth. It cheeped once before she chomped. Feathers grew from between her grinning teeth.

THE WHOREHOUSE THAT JACK BUILT

Hail Mary full of grace... and yes he could easily picture this Vestal whore as some gnostic perversion of the Divine Mother, could picture her vast belly full of life.

The albino shoved the fist of his glans into the fat of her belly, not counting on luck to find her sex but preparing to stick her again and again, like exploring for oil. The sensation on his cock was a rubbery squeezing, sweat and dead skin forming a slimy lubricant. He kept pushing, the pressure of her fat folds squeezing him harder, and shoving inch after inch of himself into the enormous folds of waste blubber. He grabbed at her for purchase, gripped moist handfuls of her obesity and her flesh spoke...

Bear-Maiden was from a tribe whose men earned honor from the fat of their wives the bigger their woman surely the greater was their skill as a hunter to provide such quantities of food a bizarre reversal of the more common Injun ritual of potlatch *her husband Coyote was a fierce warrior whose reputation grew even as his wife did and as she grew so did her greed and as she grew so did his desire for more honour and the two hungers devoured each other...*

Two thirds of his cock was in before it pressed against anything solid.

The albino glanced up at her. Her face was five feet from his across the expanse of her bulk, and she was still eating, blood and fur slathered around her chops

"Palest face tries to arrow Bear–Maiden's navel with his mighty totem. This is heap big amusing to Bear-Maiden. Palest face cannot fill Bear-Maiden like Bear-Maiden's husband Coyote. Coyote knew how to satisfy his woman."

Whatever the albino was pressed up against suddenly gave, and three inches of his cock sank into... something wrong. Like punching through a hymen, only this was surely no hymen. The sensation was so wrong the albino pushed away from her, pulling the length of himself out of her flesh.

He looked down at his cock, wondering why he felt so sticky, and knowing he had not come could not understand why he was sheathed in lumpy yellow slime.

The lumps were moving.

His penis was covered in pus and maggots. The pus stank of rotten fish.

Disgusted, he wiped at himself, pulling sticky skeins of filth off his giant cock, his fingers webbing together. The maggots reared up, tiny red jaws twitching as they bit at him.

Bear-Maiden laughed and laughed, her necklace of ears flapping with each laugh, rolling timbers of dark amusement as she lifted a fold of fat under her breast to expose weeping sores seething with grubs. Her whole body was riddled with them, the filthy skin of the rolls rubbing and irritating until it bled and the flies came to lay eggs in the moist sores.

The albino had shoved his cock into a hive of pupae, nesting in the rotten core of the whore's navel.

He frantically wiped his cock, wincing when the maggots bit him, gripping their bodies between thumb and finger to twist them off before they started drinking his blood. Hardened against all the fluids of pleasure, still even he was repulsed by what Bear-Maiden represented; like a ripe gourd apparently bulging with life, she was in fact wholly decayed within.

THE WHOREHOUSE THAT JACK BUILT

His near-permanent erection dipped a little, such was his disgust.

All thoughts of the Holy Mother went from his mind. He could not fantasise this creature of death had anything in common with the divine belly swollen with Childe that normally stoked his desire.

In a rare moment in which his ego surfaced, the albino felt pure hate. Something of the rare emotion must have shown in his eyes, because the whore stopped laughing when next she gazed down at him over her expanse.

Stopped laughing with her mouth still open... and that was when he knew where the Gash was. Where else could it be, but stitched inside the orifice her life had revolved about?

The albino reached for his holsters like a gunfighter going for his irons, but instead of pulling twin revolvers he produced the Crucifux, two long, blackened chunks of wood almost the size and shape of his own cock.

A pair of dildos carved from pieces of the true cross.

He held them out at right angles to one another, forming the symbol of faith.

The Injun whore hissed and tried to shield her eyes; the symbol hurt her twice, both as a demon and as a redskin whose tribe and culture had been decimated by the white man bearing it as an excuse for genocide.

"Oh pity Bear–Maiden, palest face," she moaned, "She has the white man's disease of spirit! Do not taunt Bear–Maiden with the symbol of that disease!"

The albino said, "Disease of spirit?"

The Injun whore grinned slyly.

"To want more than you need," she said, "To have *eyes* bigger than your *belly.*"

She cackled.

The albino swung a Crucifux high and plunged it into the whore's belly, sinking it deep into the rotten flesh, and then stabbed the other into a blubbery roll above the first. The smell of the bloody fat that squirted out was spoiled eggs.

The whore screamed.

The albino pulled himself up the side of her bulk, keeping a grip on one of the Crucifux as he pulled the other free, swinging it high again and ramming it deep into her right tit. She screamed, and he had another handhold to haul himself up.

As he climbed the disgusting obesity towards her face his body was pressed against her rotten-meat stinking flesh and it spoke...

Bear-Maiden's tribe believed in the wendigo an insane spirit of the long winter nights possessed of an insatiable appetite for human flesh a spirit of slaughter and madness a spirit possessed of insatiable apetitie a spirit of possession.

She squealed and shuddered, her wasted muscles unable to move her body enough to shake him off as the albino crawled up her slimy body towards her mouth, stabbing handholds for himself with the divine sex toys.

There came a brutal winter that forced the whole tribe to shelter all in her husband's long house it had been a hard Autumn food ran low and was rationed and one evening out of the cold waste came the foul spirit of appetite KILL THEM EAT THEM who spoke to Bear-Maiden's greed and to her husband Coyote's desire and when spring came only one remained in the long house, better fed than even in her husband's prime EAT EAT EAT.

The miracle she was a perversion of he saw very clearly as clearly as he saw what took place in that dark and frozen long house tribal elders friends relatives cousins and parents killed by Coyote and fed to Bear-Maiden EAT THEM ALL and his last act was self-slaughter to feed his ever hungry wife the miracle of the feasting on the five thousand.

The albino was on her chest. He stabbed one of the Crucifux down into her collar, blood laced yellow fat spurted out. She swatted at him, but her arms had no strength, her blows were nothing.

The albino was on his knees on her chest, one hand gripping the dildo spearing her collar-flesh, the other held above his head. His cock stood righteous and hard before her face, quivering with the pulse of his heart.

Bear-Maiden tried to look at him around the massive column of flesh, but when she did she saw the hatred in his eyes, eyes still full of the vision her flesh spoke.

"Even the children... such a *waste...*" he said, and smashed her teeth in with the other Crucifux, a club to her mouth once, twice, thrice.

She howled and clawed at his thighs.

The albino wasn't done.

Kneeling and sunk thigh deep in the mass of her chest he pulled the other Crucifux free of her shoulder and raised them both above his head; he slammed them both down into her eyes, the dildos blunt ends bursting the orbs and stabbing through the sockets deep into her brain.

She screamed. It hurt the albino's ears, but only for a moment; the wide oval of burst gums from which the scream ululated was an open invitation, and now anchored he rammed the entire thirteen inches of his arm thick erection straight down the whore's throat. His swollen scrotum mashed against her chins as he slammed his pelvis up against her lips, feeling the length of himself squeezing into the tube of the Injun whore's gullet.

Panicking, her bloody gums mashed around him, clamped down as if to bite through the engorged rope of meat, but the pressure was only pleasurable and the cutting of blood flow made his veins swell up all along the shaft.

Half kneeling, hands tight around the impaling dildos, the albino rapidly bucked his hips, letting half a foot of cock slide up before shoving it back down again, and again, and again.

What goes into the mouth...

Bear-Maiden raked at his legs and buttocks, clawing up furrows of bleeding skin. Her body shuddered in what he thought were agony-spasms, but then realised were not; she was gagging.

No sooner did the albino realise this then the whore puked.

The rush of vomit exploded up her throat, squeezing the narrow spaces around his cock, and blasted into his lap in a hose of bile and chewed-up raw meat. Her overstuffed belly reacted to the gag reflex of his giant cock in her gullet by blowing everything she had eaten, the pressure making it spray out around the massive erection filling her mouth.

THE WHOREHOUSE THAT JACK BUILT

Vomit splattered up his chest, across his face. The albino closed his eyes against the chunky, sour stomach-sewage, sealing his lips tight and turning his head to stop it getting up his nostrils. He dry swallowed a little bile of his own, but he neither let go of the Crucifux impaled into the whore's face nor stopped bucking his hips; the sensation of the gut-slurry rushing up around his slickened shaft, the lubricated feeling of fucking a puke stuffed throat... his balls contracted and he roared as he blew his fuck in a massive orgasm.

In the seconds of weakness after release the whore moved; her hands swung out widly, punching him in the heart, and helped by the surging tide of vomit she was spewing she shoved the albino backwards, distracted in his post-come glow.

He pitched over, his bare back slapping against the vomit soaked belly of the whore and sending him slide-tumbling down her fat rolls to crash to the ground winded.

The second stolen gash had to have been in her throat... and yet she still lived. The albino breathed shallowly, trying to understand how his guess could have been wrong; where could the gash have been if not down her throat?

Bear-Maiden's hands were gripping the ends of the Crucifux's that stuck out of her eyesockets. With a warrior's cry she pulled the dildos out of her skull, the sacred wooden phallusses streaked with brains, and threw them aside.

She stared sightless down at the albino, and even as meat-vomit continued to flow from her mouth so it began to burp out of her ruined eyes. Animal guts and stomach acid rolled down her cheeks and rage contorted her mouth, her lips drawing back from pulpy gums that began to sprout white needles, vicious new teeth pushing through.

"*Eeacheeewww... eeeattt yoooouuuu...*" moaned the whore in the voice of the wendigo, the voice of hunger and madness.

Across the vast expanse of Bear-Maiden's belly strange shapes moved. No, not across, but beneath, faces pressed up from beneath her skin, from within her obesity, old faces, young faces, faces mouthing unheard screams and pleas.

The feasting of the five thousand... the trapped spirits of her tribe, the tribe her husband had murdered in the cabin-fever madness of the wendigo and fed to her.

Hands reached out from behind the rubbery skin, clutching.

The albino felt a tiny pang of compassion; those savages had died without being saved by the blood of the Nazarene, could never know repentance, and were trapped forever in their special corner of Hell.

The faces stopped seething beneath the skin, now only reaching hands groped from behind the curtain of slimy fat which was the Vestal's bloated belly. Hands that reached out towards him and then descended to slap flat against the floor... it was like watching the undulating feet of a centipede, and inch by inch the whore began to crawl forwards.

"*EEEEEAAAAAATT YOOOOOOOUUUUUU....*" she groaned, vomit flowing from her mouth and eyes and down her cheeks and chins. Flowing over her necklace of severed ears.

...but what comes out of the mouth...

The albino was on his feet and was backing away from the whore. As the hands of the devoured reached out against the elastic resistance of skin and clawed at him they were not only moving the mountain of flesh forward, but were turning her over like a ball; she was rolling not crawling, her head slowly tilting towards him, teeth gnashing. She belched and ropes of puke exploded from her eyes. Her vast, shapeless tits began to sag forward over the rolls of her gut, her nipples hanging like stalagmites.

He kept stepping backwards as she rolled towards him on dozens of hands, thinking fast. *What goes into a man's mouth does not make him unclean, but what comes out of his mouth, that is what makes him unclean.* The necklace of ears that was almost choking her, nearly vanishing between one ballooning chin and the next.

(what comes out of the mouth; words, not vomit)

(unclean words. Heard)

The albino was backed against a wall.

Eyeless face, mouth crowded with teeth, descending slowly as a setting moon as sure as a nightmare.

The albino rubbed his cock with one hand, encouraging the blood to flow thicker, faster, stiffening to full mast again.

"*EEEEEAAAAAATTT YYYOOOOOOOOUUUUUU...*"

When the Injun's face was three feet above him he grabbed at the necklace, fingers slipping into the tight binding and pulling hard, snapping the sinew it was tied with.

The whore's chins blossomed open like a flower, meat folds parting, no longer bound shut; not a flower, a pussy. The second stolen gash. Throat worn with swallowing tons of flesh, devouring life in an orgy of disgusting greed, gulping down muscle and organs and splintered bones, a hole rubbed through the cartilage and now patched with the vivisected cunt of a Whitechapel prostitute.

Bear–Maiden's teeth snapped at his face.

The albino shoved his hand into the whore's mouth and grabbed her tongue; her teeth gnashed down on the rosary wound about his wrist, unable to bite through the sanctified metal links. Lightning swift he twisted his free hand into her headdress and pulled himself up, swinging his legs up to wrap around her neck and thrusting his crotch upwards to skewer the pussy in her gullet with his erection. He clung to her and began to rut wildly, felt the tip of his cock burst up the back of her throat into her sinuses. He felt the whore roaring, felt her vocal chords vibrating against his shaft.

Yes; this was the second keyhole. He could perform the sexorcism, break the lock and seal the gate.

"Lorem ipsum dolor sit amet," the albino chanted wrapping his legs ever tighter around the Vestal's neck as he rutted upside down hands white knuckled with his grip on her hair and tongue her teeth champed upon the rosary now in pain and terror, knowing she was doomed, still trying to scream and only arousing him further, "Consectetur adipisicing elit, sed do eiusmod tempor incididunt ut labore et dolore magna aliqua," fucking her gullet he felt the hyoid bone snap the bone that holds the windpipe in place felt it snap like the wishbone from a turkey, "Ut enim ad minim veniam, quis nostrud exercitation ullamco laboris nisi ut aliquip ex ea commodo consequat," and he pictured his cock stuffed down the whore's throat and he remembered the sensation of high pressure vomit lubricating him and that was enough, "Duis aute irure dolor in reprehenderit in voluptate velit esse cillum dolore eu fugiat nulla pariatur, excepteur sint occaecat cupidatat non proident, sunt in culpa qui OFFICIA deserunt MOLLIT anim ID EST LABORUM... AMEN!" He yelled and blew his fuck his semen thundering up his shaft to exploded in her sinuses like a geyser and twin jets blasted from her nostrils like snot cleaning out the last traces of her puke.

She convulsed and he clutched her tight, letting the aftershocks of the orgasm shake him. Finally he relaxed his grip and slid his legs from around her neck, his cock sliding out of the cunt in her throat, his feet settling back onto the ground.

Her teeth were still clamped around his wrist, still crunched against the rosary wrapped around his wrist. He let go of her headdress and pulled at her lower jaw, separating her teeth enough to let his other hand slide free and as he did so he saw the fire in her goat eyes dwindle to embers, and die.

He used two fingers to close the whore's eyes, made the sign of the cross on her forehead.

"Requiem in pace," he muttered.

Bear-Maiden's corpse, rested on its enormous belly, shuddered and shivered.

The albino frowned. Her whole purpose was to serve as a host for one of the keyholes, for her body to provide an entry into the world of flesh for the Enemy. When the albino had fucked the gash he had broken the Rite of Passage, and with her purpose gone Hell would no longer animate her erectoplasmic body.

But still she shuddered.

Then they started to emerge; the maggots, the grubs, the worms and pupa that had nested in the decaying folds, in the weeping sores that had fed them. Like rats deserting a sinking ship, the parasites wriggled out of the sweaty, stinking rolls of fat and dropped to the floor to squirm mindlessly.

And then the corpse shit itself, a Judgement day trumpet of a fart blasting through the lard pillows of flab which were her ass, a trumpet that turned wet at the end as a whale spout of brown rope exploded from between the rolls of fat.

An omen of what was to come.

CHAPTER IV

"Not as Cain, who was of that Wicked One, and slew his brother."

John 3:12

(In the Garden how many were there that went on two legs there were three that went on two legs Adam and Eve and the Other.

(Who is the Son of God He is His own Son.

(What was its name that was the Other the Other in the garden was called the Serpent.

(Who was the mother of God the Virgin Mary was the mother of God.

(It is written that Adam knew Eve but once, yet how many children she bore Eve knew Adam once, but she bore two children.

(And who was the wife of the Son of God the Whore Mary was His wife.)

The turd lay on a white cloth upon the Altar of Cloacina. It was a foot long and stone-heavy.

The albino and the Motherfucker Superior both knelt beside the toilet. As the Church had done with many other pagan deities, it *had absorbed the Roman Goddess of the sewers for itself, and made of her one of the aspects of the Holy Mother.*

No lesson at the seminary was ever simple.

"At the gates of life and death we are companied by it," said the Motherfucker Superior, "In the moments after we are born, it is there; at our final breath, it is there. Like sin, though we shun it all our lives, it is with us every day. What is it?"

She picked the turd up with reverence, holding it in both hands like an offering.

The albino had to carefully assemble what hints she portioned out with his own knowledge, gleaned from his hours of silent study in the Vatican's libraries, poring over texts of theology, philosophy, medicine, phytogeography, the lore of metaphysics...

"In the moments after we are born..." said the albino, "Immediately after childbirth the mother experiences an autonomous bowel movement, her body attempting to pass on gut microbes to the new-born whose intestines have no healthy intestinal flora? In the moments after we are born our mother defecates on us."

The Motherfucker Superior watched him over the turd, her ancient, rheumy eyes piercing him.

"At our final breath..." said the albino, "At the moment of true death the body relaxes and the guts empty for the last time?"

He said; "Shit. The answer is shit."

The Motherfucker Superior nodded.

"This is one of our most holy relics," she told the albino, "Recovered by Mary from the foot of the cross after the Redeemer was carried from Golgotha. This is the final mortal act of Jesus."

THE WHOREHOUSE THAT JACK BUILT

And then she offered it to him.

At first he was at a loss for what to do with it. He was the only true male in the order; unlike the nuns he could not fuck himself with the holy turd. But in a moment it was clear to him; of course he could receive the relic within himself.

He bent over and carefully shoved the length of the hard, ancient faeces up his rectum. When the tapered end nudged his prostate he groaned and came and the albino's eyes were opened even further.

*

An armadillo was being fucked in the ass by a raccoon whilst a grizzly bear watched and masturbated, his grizzly bear erection wrapped in one paw.

The room the albino had stepped into was a shack, a backwoods cabin filled with the art of a perverted taxidermist. Everywhere were mangy stuffed animals posed in sex acts with one another, carnal relations between predator and prey? A snapping turtle was being fellated by a rattlesnake. A wolf was being raped by wolverines. A turkey was sodomising a bald eagle.

And instead of stuffed and mounted heads hanging on the walls were the genitals of almost every kind of fauna that the United States could boast.

In one corner of the room an ancient stove provided light, and besides this greasy curtains hung from a wood pole in the roof. The sleeping area was sectioned off by these curtains, and something stirred behind them, and called out;

"Yooooo hoooooo..." and this was followed by a long, loud fart.

The sound was so unexpected in that place that it caught him off guard, reached down into the place where any semblance he had of a personality had been repressed since his earliest memories, and the albino laughed. The simple, most childish reaction any human can have to that most fundamental and childish of sounds.

Trained like a dog to associate happiness with agony, the simple joy of laughing at a rude noise drove a corkscrew of pain through his brain; it snapped him to attention, twisted the rosary tighter about his wrist, slapped the gun holsters where the Crucifux hung ready, and tugged at his cock to make sure it stood stiff and ready for the third Vestal whore.

A head poked from between the curtains.

Freckled, straw wild hair, gap toothed, and chinless, but far too young to be a grandmother. She couldn't have been more than seventeen. He'd been expecting a crone, not some backwoods nymph.

"Well lookee here, I'se gots me a gennelman calluh!" said *Grandma* Spuckler, "Hmmm! Kinda scrawny peckerwood, ain'cha? An' ain'chu never seen the sun?"

The head tilted, looked down his body and stopped at his waist.

She clucked her tongue.

" Lordy! No wunder ya got sent to me! That there is some passel of man-meat! Shit, wuz y'daddy a fuckin' mule?"

The albino said nothing, just stood with his erection pointing towards her.

The girl frowned.

"I ast y'a civil question, peckerwood. Jus' cuz y'sold y'soul ta fuck me doan't excuze bad manners," her head tilted to one side, the curtains still pinched closed around her neck, "Or mebbe yer a mute? That it? Y'deaf 'n' dumb, cain't hear me, cain't speak?"

The albino shook his head.

"So y'kin hear me, but kin y'speak?"

The albino nodded.

"Righ'. So, whut? Cat got yer tongue or is y'jest rude?"

The albino said;

"Why are you called grandma?"

The girl laughed. The gaps in her teeth were wide enough to push fingers through.

"A'cuz that's whut I is, dummy!"

Behind the curtain something big moved and there came enough tremendous farts.

The albino gritted his teeth, willed himself to ignore it.

"Why," she said, grinning, "I's all kinds of things! I's a grandmaw, an' I'se a niece, an' I's a sister an' a daughter an' a couzin an' an aunt an' I's myself too! I's one big, happy fambly!"

She parted the curtains and she rose from her cot and stumbled out into the room.

Mary Maggie Darling had too many holes, and this had too many holes. Bear-Maiden had too much flesh, and this had too much flesh. The thing called Grandma Spuckler was surely a demon from some obscure corner of the Depths, because nothing human could be so... and still live.

Above the waist she was any typical backwoods nymph, the kind jealously guarded by brothers and uncles, all tits and freckles, from one of those families who spoke of George Washington as *King Washington*, and lived in rotting shacks that were ancient before the revolution. But below the waist she was fabulous. Three centuries of inbreeding...

The albino thought of an octopus, centipede, spider kind of thing, or some awful offspring of such critters, broken insects writhing and twitching. She was normal to the waist, but then instead of legs she grew into a pair of torsos oddly fused together, and from these grew more conjoined trunks, chests and bellies, and all of these extra part-bodies had arms and legs and orifices. The albino thought of a potato lousy with eyes, buried, other potatoes budding off from it and growing and budding; she was an insane tree root tangle of tumours and muscles that twitched spasmodically, boneless arms with foot long webbed fingers, spindly legs with three, four, five joints that ended in triple toed paws.

A dozen anuses gaped from within the mass, red and raw. One of them farted, the sore skin rippling as an eggy blast blew across the room.

Somehow she stood upright upon this train of mutated flesh.

"Y'all ever hear tell o'them *Si-am-ese* twins?" she said, "Like they have up in them travellin' shows? Bodies all mixed t'gether so y'caint make out where one starts an' t'other ends?"

The albino knew what she spoke of. Amongst the hordes of the Vatican's sex slaves there were a group of concubines from the traditional Roman circus; pinheads, dwarfs, lobster girls, and even, yes, Siamese twins. The Lamore twins. In his training the albino had fucked them both, at once; they shared a rectum, amongst other body parts. They had even been purchased from one of the shows the whore had spoken of, the *Edward Gnash & Son's Show of Splendours.*

Grandma Spuckler grinned.

"Well, I's a Si-am-ese twin too... and three sets of Si-am-ese triplets t'boot! Shit, fella, I's a one woman orgy!"

Laughing, she slumped backwards onto the cot and threw all her limbs up, offering a dozen different entrances into the mess of her body.

"So c'mon fella! Howsabout y'all get y'self over here wit tha' big ol' pole o'yours and *fuck mah brains out?*"

Of what miracle of the Nazarene was she some terribly perversion? The albino saw at once; the Gadarene demoniac, the man of Gadarene who was infested with some many demons that they called themselves Legion. The Redeemer had cast them out; in his training the albino had read in the Gospel of Mary the precise nature of the Rite of Sexorcism Christ used, sodomy followed by forcing the demoniac to suck his own shit off the Shepard's Rod. Legion had fled into a nearby herd of pigs, considering the animals cleaner than the humans.

I am Legion we are many.

I's a one woman orgy!

The demoniac was one flesh possessed by countless demons.

The Vestal was countless flesh with a single demon soul.

The albino breathed deeply, trying to fix his mind on an erotic image that would provide focus whilst he fucked this abomination. As ever, the Holy Mother was uppermost in his mind, her belly swollen with Childe... but the third Vestal whore crossed and uncrossed her lower limbs and it was like crabs or spiders eating too many segmented appendages twitching and the albino knew he'd need more to fantasise about if he was to sexorcise this thing.

He thought of choir boys.

Another pagan tradition the Church had devoured and made its own; the demand that the local population sacrifice a number of virgins to it every season.

Though not a priest, the thought of unsuspecting and trusting young flesh was enough to harden his resolve, cock swelling to full-mast, veins prominent and pulsing with his heartbeat as blood pumped into the vast organ.

The dozen shit caked anuses gaping clod-mouthed before him could be the rumps of a dozen peasent children, drunk on communion wine and not likely to remember this...

The albino chose a hole at random, felt bizarre limbs twine around him in welcome, and pushed the tip of his cock into a sore looking orifice with hard nuggets and nodules around its mouth. They scraped him, crumbled into shit dust; the inside of the anus was just as encrusted, painful to push into. He only got a third of himself in before the resistence of tight, dry membranes stopped him.

Skin touching skin he saw...

Oh momma yew taste so goooooddd oh pee-paw yew suck so goooooddd (oh pee-paw hev yew bin fuckin' mah lil boy-brother in th'ass agin doan chew lie teh me ah kin taste his shit on yer cock) oh lil brother jes' yew show yer sister whut yew kin dooooo oh my lil boy momma's so proud o' her biiiigggg boy oh mee-maw ow doan bite s'haaarrrrdddd oh dadddddddyyyyyyy (a'course it's okay doan it say righ' in th' Good Book how God was his own daddy?)

Blasphemy...

"Aww, fella, is I a mite dry down there?" asked the whore, looking down over her knees and elbows and her splayed open swaying webbed feet and warty fingers, "Tell y'whut, howsabout I make things nice an' slippery for ya? Truth to tell I's got me a *powerful* bellyache... Must be why I caint quit fartin'!"

The albino felt the various limbs twined around him suddenly grip tightly; malformed hands gripped his ankles, calves with double jointed knees wrapped around his hips and shoulders, boneless flippers hugged him tight.

Between most of these warped appendages gaped an asshole. Most often a cunt and an anus had simply run together to create one wide, brown stained ring piece; one of the largest was in front of the albino's face.

The smell of decaying eggs hissed out of it, a queef-fart.

"Oh boy!" said the Vestal, hands gripping her belly, just above where her body suddenly blossomed into so many half formed twins and triplets of herself, the octopus thrashing mass in which the albino was caught, "Oh boy, oooooh, this is gunna be one o' those hot ones! UHHHNNNNNNNNGGGHH!"

She strained. Her stomach grumbled, whined, gurgled. Her face turned red and the albino struggled to free himself before she blew but it was no good and she screeched in triumph as she shit herself every anus surrounding him farted wetly and gushed.

Hot, semi-solid faeces burped from each anus, mud-fudge chunks in a caramel sludge streaked with bloody traces of stomach lining. The albino, held in place, could only thrash his head as the slurry exploded from the asses around him; he clamped his eyes and mouth shut as the paste thickened with clods splattered his face. Wet flecks got up his nostrils and the stench of sour guts flooded his sinuses. He could almost taste it, and a sudden bile-flavoured belch of disgust nearly caused him to open his mouth. The legs and arms and hands and feet around him became slick with shit and his own skin was smeared as the weird limbs tried to maintain their ever slippery grip on him. He felt the ass his cock was jammed into straining to blow its contents against the blockage of his erection, and the sensation of chunky shit squeezing between the anus wall and his foreskin was like the sensation of fucking Bear-Maiden's throat as she puked. The lubrication meant he was sliding in further even as Spuckler strained to shit against him and he felt his arousal growing so much that he gasped with pleasure and his mouth was instantly filled.

Almost worse than the taste was the texture flooding across his tongue and against his teeth, oatmeal-soil with chunks.

He swallowed. It was that or choke.

His belly rebelled but held its peace, trained for years in the seminary to accept whatever horrors were fed to it, practical lessons that followed careful study of the standard theological work on excremental, *On the Origin of Faeces.*

The way that burst pipes will slow to a trickle when the pressure is gone so did the whore's anuses gradually shrink as the flood of shit shrank and tapered off into a chorus of wet farts.

"Hooooooo, boy!" crowed the whore, "I sure needed that! Hmmm!"

The albino scraped at his face, wiping the worst of the shit from his eyes and mouth, pressing a thumb to each nostril and blowing them clean, but the anus his cock was still lodged in was now slippery enough for him to fuck properly and like a horse that leads itself to its stable his hips were already thrusting his thirteen inches deep into her.

"Yeah, c'mon boy, fuck mah brains out!" the whore laughed.

The limbs grip on him had relaxed so he grabbed an ankle and a wrist, gripped tight, and then he really began to give it to her.

The albino was picturing dirty faced choir boys opening their mouths to accept communion, their eyes closed as he masturbated, both his hands wrapped around the giant rope of his penis, gripping it hard as he savagely pumped his length and prepared to blow his fuck all over their...

The anus in front of his face farted like someone blowing a raspberry with a mouth full of refried beans, pebble dashing his face.

He lost his rhythm, his fantasy perverted.

"'Scuze me preacher, guess I ain't finished yet!"

Coils and loops of stringy shit spurted from the anus and across the albino's face.

He grabbed one of the Crucifux from his right holster faster than any gunslinger at high noon and rammed the blessed dildo into the spluttering hole plugging the turds.

"Hey, that's cheatin'!" said the whore; her face screwed up in concentration and she grunted and suddenly an anus to his left ringed by five stuump-arms like a starfish coughed a shotgun blast of droppings at him.

The albino drew the other Crucifux and stabbed the asshole with it, shoving up to the hilt against the hail of feces.

"Unnngggh..." groaned the whore.

He lifted his left foot and stuffed it up an asshole, then plugged another asshole with his right foot, before punching a fist into yet another. Securely anchored he started to thrust again, dismissing the choir boys as too old, imagining instead the Blessed Mother round and huge with Childe, concentrating as hard on blowing his fuck.

"Ha! Y'all ran out of ways to plug me up afore I ran outta holes, huh preacher?" leered Grandma Spuckler, grinning with all the teeth gingivitis hadn't taken.

The albino pictured the Virgin cunt, hymen straining with the foetus of the Christ Childe, saw himself licking at the thin membrane, all that separated him from...

His cock throbbed dangerously. His huge balls ached, readying themselves.

He dug his feet in deeper into their holes and clenched his fists; in none of his limbs did he feel the tell-tale sparks of dark energy which suggested any contained the Gash he had to seal.

But he could at least eliminate them.

THE WHOREHOUSE THAT JACK BUILT

The swollen belly of the Virgin and the Childe inside kicked as if it too yearned...

The albino cried out in orgasm as he blew an enormous quantity of fuck into the whore's shit slick asshole. His cries were joined by yelps from the third Vestal whore as his Holy Spunk seared her insides as he pumped and pumped and pumped more and more into her.

"Oh shit preacher whut t'fuck is wrong wit' yer cock snot!" screeched Grandma Spuckler.

A foot lashed out and kicked the albino in the jaw; boneless fingers scrabbled and slapped at his chest; elbows and knees pressed against his belly, trying to pry him off, but still he clung on and continued to thrust.

"Giddoff me! Giddoff me! Ahhhh fuck, it burrnnnnsss..."

Through the bizarre plumbing of Grandma Spuckler's siamese parts divine semen flowed like white lava, scorching and searing through interconnected rectums and guts... to squirt out unplugged assholes in geysers of shit streaked holy cream.

The albino grunted under the assault of the whore's flailing limbs, his mind clearing, and began to pull himself out of the whore; he pulled his rosary wrapped wrist and fist out with a wet pop and a gush of cum and diarrhoea, then pulled out the Crucifux with twin sucking sounds from anuses that vomited sticky strings of spunk and soft raisins of shit.

No longer restrained by the hands and feet that instead were frantically beating he let himself fall backwards from the tangle and his feet slid easy out of greasy assholes that began to weep clotted filth. He hit the floor and rolled

Spuckler wailed and thrashed as delicate membranes burned, bubbling and blistering as if the gluey semen were acid.

The albino got to his feet slowly, watching.

He glanced from hole to hole to hole between frantically waving legs and arms, barely noticing Spuckler cussing him out from between gritted teeth, her goat eyes turning black.

The anus closest to her belly where her body turned into a mass of twisted torsos and limbs was not weeping with his seed, the only organ that was not.

Back into the fray the albino waded back into the tangle of limbs, grunting when kicked or slapped, using the half formed torsos as stepping stones to clamber closer to Spuckler's main trunk. The hole that did not leak was roughly where her left shin should have been, right in the centre of a chest, between tits.

"Fuck y'preacher!" spat the whore, "Y'might have burned me all up but I's made o' erectoplasm, and I's gunna heal up, but y'ain't never gunna be able to fuck mah brains out! Y'might've worn out mah sisters, but y'ain't gittin' outta mah room in one piece, I promise y'that!"

The albino clambered over a leg that split into two calves at the knee, both ending in eight toed feet, and he was at the hole.

Spuckler smacked and slapped at the top of his head

"Geddoff, that'un ain't fur you! That'un is fur Mistuh Marshall!"

The albino grabbed the whore's flailing hands and quickly bound her wrists with his rosary. She goggled at his speed; gagging and binding were some of the first lessons taught at the seminary.

THE WHOREHOUSE THAT JACK BUILT

One hand holding the rosary binding her wrists, using her arms as an anchor, the albino turned his attention to the anus or cunt or... now he was closer he was uncertain what this strange opening in the Siamese flesh was. Nothing in his training had prepared him for this, and with his free hand he stroked his semi-erect penis and studied the thing.

It was like a half open flower made of meat. The petals looked like tongues, curled in on themselves; he directed the tip of his cock down and teased it around and around them, and they uncurled and they *were* tongues, opening up just as a flower will in the morning sun, to reveal an orifice that was like a choked throat lined with eyeballs, lash less lids blinking up at him.

"No y'don't, that's fur Mistah Marshall!" the whore yammered, trying to tug her wrists back, though the albino held firm, "He made that a'special cuz I's his fav'rit! He tole me so!"

The albino spat in his free hand and began working his cock hard again, feeling his inexhaustible balls swelling again with more Holy Spunk. Once again, an emotion played within him, an emotion that like love and laughter and every other had been beaten and raped out of him since his earliest memory.

He was excited.

He was excited at the thought of performing what was otherwise his sacred duty. After years of training, of every day violating mouths and asses and cunts, of growing so desensitised to hideous flesh and wicked fluids, here was something genuinely new to stick his cock into; he had sexorcised demons on three different continents, but ultimately no matter how bestial or bizarre they may have been, there were only so many possible confirgurations of genitalia.

A cunt lined with eyeballs and rimmed with tongues; he'd fucked plenty that had teeth, but never eyes... and it truly excited him.

He didn't even care if it contained the Gash he was supposed to seal.

He stuffed the purple head of his cock into the weird orifice, groaning when the tongues clapped around his shaft, lubricating his length as he slowly forced inch after inch of his cock in. The eyeballs that lined the throat or cunt added a second fluid; saliva was familiar to the skin of his erection, but tears were novel... and even as he eased himself in he felt the eyes blinking, rapid twitching skin on his skin like dozens of insect kisses along the length of his shaft.

She took all of him, all the way to the hilt, her tongues lapping at his balls as eyes in the meat opened and closed against the tight, sensitive skin of his glans.

In a part of his mind cool and detached from the base animal instincts the albino's training told him he was in a dangerous place, giving himself to pleasure in the course of performing his duty. But how could he not? This orifice was not just the work of some cacodaemon chirurgeon, but was the personal design of the flesh architect...

Temptation. First among the tools of demons.

He sawed his hips slowly, allowing almost his entire foot long cock to slide back out of the orifice before he plunged himself back in again, over and over. There was no complaint from Grandma

Spuckler; her breathing was shallow, her eyes were closed but fluttering and her many limbs stirred in slow ecstasy. Evidently the experience was good for her as well.

The albino groaned. He was allowing himself to enoy this.

One of Grandma Spuckler's eyes opened and looked at the albino fucking her with such abandon, and grinned a sly grin.

"Uhhhnn, yeah, sweet thin'," she moaned, her grin attesting that her pleasure was feigned, "Oooooh shit, preacher, thass so gooooddd..."

The albino was gone. Temptation had won out over his training, and now he was a beast, humping for no other reason than his basic animal lust.

Hell held its breath.

The albino's grip on the whore's bound hands threatened to pull her arms out of their sockets as he thrust. He ground against her and slowly pulled out, relishing the way the tongues seemed to try and prevent him pulling free, dragging over his skin as if seeking purchase, and then suddenly thrusting again, his girth squeezing against the open eyes that lined the throat, eyes that closed like slimy mouths against his skin.

"Uhhhnnnn, yea', thass it," the whore moaned in fake pleasure, "Gimme all y'got preacher, gimme *everythin'*...

Every drop.

There was a quickening, nerves lighting up one by one like those new electric candles as he built towards another climax, but one unlike any he had had so far in The Half-World; this one would be given wholly for pleasure, and would damn him.

"Yeeeaaahhh!" whooped Grandma Spuckler, "Fuck me! Yeah preacher, unnhhh! Shit, preacher, y'r even better at layin' pipe than mah cuzzin bruther!"

 The albino thrashed against her.

"Now call me baby gurl!" cried the whore, "C'mawn, call me y'r baby girl just like mah paw-paw!"

The words instantly cut through the albino's lust-fugue.

"Baby... girl?" he echoed.

The whore frowned, wondering why he had suddenly stopped hopping up and down in her like a mole rat in a pail of slugs.

"Baby..." he muttered, the fugue dissipating, his mind clearing, the awful realization dawning that he had almost been lost, "Girl?"

A baby girl was not how his fantasy ran, not at all, not a female.

Not the Childe.

The effect was instant; moments before he had been ready to blow his final fuck in one last orgasm, one last little death that would have lasted seconds and been regretted for eternity... and the sudden reminder to his consciousness that he was reaming out a demon *bitch* stopped everything, like a sledge to a steer's head.

His cock twitched as the eyes fluttered deep in the meat, blinking as fast as a dreamer in a nightmare, desperate to urge him over the edge.

He started to pull out, the tongues lapping at him desperately.

"Hey noaw, preacher," said the whore, "Hey noaw, wha'chu think y'r doin', preacher? Y'all gotta fuck me! Y'all gotta make me cream, preacher! Huh?"

The albino shook his head, slowly, side to side, and slid inch after inch out of her weird hole.

"Naw, naw, naw!" she cried, yanking her arms up closer to her chest, dragging him forward even as he pulled his hips back, "Naw, y'ain't dun here preacher! Y'ain't had y'r fill yet! C'mawn, fuck me!" and pleading turned instantly to insults, "T'fuck is wrong wit'chu, preacher? Ain'chu a man? A man'ud stick me but good! A man'ud make me scream! A man, why, a real man'ud fuck mah brains out!"

The tip of his cock, a fist covered in tears and spit, eased out of the hole, lapped by the tongues until the last, clear and stick fluids dripping down like decaying spiderwebs.

The albino tightened his grip on the rosary binding her wrists, steadying himself to lunge at her.

In the instant before he did their eyes met; and she saw that he knew.

Fuck mah brains out.

He was faster.

In a moment he was on top of Grandma Spuckler, on the half of her above the waist that was only one person and not the half-aborted remains of a half dozen others. She tried to thrash him off, but with her hands bound and her lower half sprawled out on the ground she was trapped, and the albino punched her in the throat.

Gasping for air, he crawled over her shoulder and grabbed her pigtails and then he was on his knes, lifting her head up with one pigtail wrapped around each fist like they were reins, revealing the back of her skull. Where the hair was gathered up to be braided together into her pigtails there was a clear parting, and in that parting hot and juicy was the stolen Gash of a Whitechapel prostitute.

"Got you," he muttered, and settled the end of his cock into the waiting folds.

"UUUHHHHNNNNAAAAAAAAAAWWWW..." hollered Grandma Spuckler, and then he pulled her pigtails like pulling a horse to a halt yanking her head back onto his crotch and his thirteen inch cock impaled her brain splitting apart the two hemispheres like hammering a nail through a walnut.

It was like fucking a haggis fresh from the oven; piercing the outer membrane that the brain was wrapped in was like spearing through the lamb's stomach into the soft, mushy filling.

He fucked her memories and dreams, the electrictrified fat of her mind, feeling the tip-top of her spinal column scraping the belly of his shaft as his balls slapped against the nape of her neck. When he drew back his cock it was smeared with the grey yolky muck of neural tissue, filth that squirted from the Gash as he shoved himself back in again.

Grandma Spuckler was gasping in a weird hitching rhythm, sometimes hiccupping, sometimes giggling or crying out like a bird, her body receiving wrong messages from the ruins of her brain. Clotted blood gushed from her sinuses and bloody tears flowed from her bulging eyes.

The albino recalled from his training that skullfucking had a heritage as old as antiquity; trepanation had been developed by early man as a primitive means of relieving pressure headaches, but should the patient not survive the cure, but who would pass up the invitation of such a hole?

THE WHOREHOUSE THAT JACK BUILT

The whore was trying to speak, but all that came out was sing-song nonsense.

"N'gai, n'gha'ghaa, bugg-shoggog, y'hah..." she gurgled.

The albino shortened his strokes and began to intone the words of the prayer of sexorcism;

"Lorem ipsum dolor sit amet..." he grunted.

"Yog-Sothoth, Yog-Sothoth..." the whore gurgled.

"Consectetur adipisicing elit, sed do eiusmod tempor incididunt ut labore et dolore magna aliqua..." gasped the albino, pounding, pounding.

"Ygnailh... ygnaiih... thflthkh'ngha.... Yog-Sothoth..." the whore's eyes were being forced further and further from her skull with each thrust of the albino's massive penis into her skull.

"Ut enim ad minim veniam, quis nostrud exercitation ullamco laboris nisi ut aliquip ex ea commodo consequat..." he muttered, concentrating on his rhytmn.

"Y'bthnk...h'ehye—n'grkdl'lh...Eh-y-ya-ya-yahaah—e'yayayaaaa... ngh'aaaaa... ngh'aaa... h'yuh... h'yuh..." the whore spluttered.

"Duis aute irure dolor in reprehenderit in voluptate velit esse cillum dolore eu fugiat nulla pariatur..." the come was bubbling, his balls aching, ready to...

Suddenly the whore began to thrash wildly, her neck whipping back and forth and side to side as a death spasm gripped her, and finally recognizably English words burst forth as the albino held tight and tried to finish.

"HELP! HELP!" screamed Grandma Spuckler, "Dd—dd—dd—DADDY! DADDY! YOG-SOTHOTH!"

The albino snapped her pigtails like reins, hard, wrapping the hair around his fists even tighter and frantically sawing into her brains as he recited the final words... "Excepteur sint occaecat cupidatat non proident, sunt in culpa qui OFFICIA deserunt MOLLIT anim ID EST LABORUM... AMEN!" And came so violently that the whore's eyes finally popped out of their cavities, forced out on a gush of pulped brains and semen.

And after only silence.

When the red-shivers left him the albino opened his eyes. For a rare moment of perspective he saw the scene as an outsider might; a man knelt upon the ground holding a woman's head in his lap, a lover who had just died in his arms.

An arm shook; a hand clenched; a leg kicked out; the spastic twitches running through her terrible body as the news of her death was carried on knotted nerves. A shudder like a wave passed through her, a rumble almost too low to hear... and then her body let go, her messed up guts and genitals queef-farting all at once, blowing bubbles of come, spraying strings and pearls into the air from a dozen holes, sticky snowfall.

An omen of what came next.

The albino pulled the whore's skull off his cock with a deep slurping sound and a flood of bloody neural tissue. He cleaned himself with her pigtails. Previous experience told him that brains itched something fierce if they dried in your pubes.

He stood, his cock swinging low and lazy at half mast, but still eager to fuck more demon flesh.

"Next."

CHAPTER V

"For I am jealous over you with godly jealousy: for I have espoused you to one husband that I may present you as a chaste virgin to Christ. But I fear, lest by any means, as the serpent beguiled Eve through his subtlety, so your minds should be corrupted..."

Corinthians 11:2-3

(In the Garden how many were there that went on two legs there were three that went on two legs Adam and Eve and the Other.

(Who is the Son of God He is His own Son.

(What was its name that was the Other the Other in the garden was called the Serpent.

(Who was the mother of God the Virgin Mary was the mother of God.

(It is written that Adam knew Eve but once, yet how many children did she bear Eve knew Adam once, but she bore two children.

(And who was the wife of the Son of God the Whore Mary was His wife.

(For whom did she bear the first child for the third in the garden.

(And why was Mary Magdalene both his mother and his wife so as to keep the line Pure of the taint of the Other.)

The Motherfucker Superior like every member of the Order of the Immaculate was a hermaphrodite. Her cock and her clitoris were the same size as one another both half a foot when flaccid and both drooped; she twisted them one about the other and had them both pierced at the end when not employed.

The symbolism was not lost on the albino. A caduceus, two snakes twined one around the other; Jacob's twisted ladder of life itself.

"The heathen Hindu's believe that it takes thirty drops of blood to create a single drop of bone marrow," said the Motherfucker Superior

All the other Sisters of the order ringed him where he knelt in the baptismal font. If he raised his eyes in any direction he would see ancient scrotums, heavy testicles swinging before the entrances of grizzled cunts. from which grotesquely bloated clitorises bloomed.

Each of the nuns began to stroke the wrinkled stalagmites of their cocks with one liver spotted hand, massaging their tumorous clits with the other. Gnarled erectile tissue and broken veins began to plump, rheumy eyes closing in bliss as each Sister began to fantasize.

THE WHOREHOUSE THAT JACK BUILT

"The heathen Hindu's believe that it takes thirty drops of bone marrow to make a single drop of semen," said the Motherfucker Superior, gasping as she too worked her ancient shepherd's rod.

The lesson seemed to have ended there, with what heathen's believed. The albino kept his peace; even heathen's could guess at the truth, and sometimes win insights.

Around him, the thirty Sisters of the Order of the Immaculate masturbated to the same fantasy. They whispered the prayer, the mantra of that fantasy, and thirty whispers were loud in that sacred place, fingers fluttering rapidly about their obscene-bloated clitorises as free palms slid back and forth along the lengths of stone-fossil erections.

The fantasy was of committing the Sacred Sin.

"Hail Mary full of grace..."

The Order was an unbroken line of descent, a colony of interbreeding hermaphrodite's who alone kept the bloodline of purity alive. Once in a generation they birthed One who was not as they, One who was complete and could go out into the world to root out the evil which aped & mocked the secret.

And their newest son was ready.

They did not all orgasm at once, but close; as each Sister imagined fucking the Childe Himself within the Divine Mother's belly, before he was born and became stained by the World, they were all joined together by the imagined Sacred Sin.

One Sister would cry out and come, spurting forth ivory streamers, and then two more would be spurred by that climax to also ejaculate great gouts of semen. They came one after another or two or three at once, enormous volumes of spunk arcing through the air, crossing paths and finally splattering across the albino's face.

His mouth was open to receive the salty issue from two and a half dozen malformed cocks, though as much was sprayed across his cheeks and eyes as he managed to guzzle.

The Motherfucker Superior held herself longest, and finally let loose with a cry of exquisite agony, her testicles hanging to her thighs and bobbing up and down as they blew a half pint of moon-pale fuck all over his lips and mouth.

The albino coughed, nearly choking; trying to swallow so much semen was like trying to swallow snot and phlegm, stickiness that needed washing down with something more fluid. Shit was easier to gag down, or even vomit if you had time to chew the chunks.

*

Flickering light from braziers made the hieroglyphics and accompanying tomb paintings seem to dance. The paintings were translations of the hieroglyphics. Beast-headed gods committed atrocities of desire upon one another, agitated by the dancing shadows.

The chamber floor was littered with mummified bodies, dry and sere from thousands of years in the cold and airless dark. Some of the mummies were big, some small, and some were child sized. All shared features in common beyond the brown flesh bound tight over their bones; wherever the albino looked he saw every orifice was violated, cunts and assholes ripped wide, teeth smashed down screaming throats... for what?

Mummies were fairly common in the West, as mouldering oddities found in travelling sideshows. But what did the architect of flesh want with meat that had been dead so long?

A memory shifted something from his studies of legends...

In the center of the chamber was a sarcophagus ringed by funerary offerings. The albino's knowledge of Egyptian burial customs was slight, but he recalled that the dead were entombed with whatever they believed they would need in the next life.

In this case, some of the most lavish sex devices he had ever seen.

The Order had the world's most extensive collection of such implements collected from every corner of the material world and the infernal dimensions, but nothing that the albino had seen or used from the collection matched these grave goods for lavishness.

Finally the name sprang to his mind with memory attendant; Clitocris. A name from myth, a story from ancient Egypt... that there was a pharoahess called Clitocris whose insatiable lust for both semen and blood cast a shadow over a whole dynasty; by dark arts she ruled for over a century, and unknown hundreds were said to have died in her bedchamber. When she finally died –stabbed, poisoned, drowned- her name was expunged from every papyrus scroll, and her hieroglyphs were erased from every obelisk and tomb. But as she was royalty she was buried with her worldly goods that they would serve her in the next life; over a thousand men, women and children formed the harem that was buried alive with the nightmare queen, to sate her lust so that she would not seek to satisfy it amongst the living.

The albino almost groaned. The dead.

He hated fucking the dead.

This Vestal Whore was an inversion of one of the greatest miracles, the promise of eternal life, resurrection.

The lid of the sarcophagus slid away and a withered hand emerged over the edge, gripping the stone to lever its owner upright. She emerged as slow as moon rise, a thing that should not be, bones and parchment flesh naked save for her death mask and the titanic thing that stuck up between her fleshless legs.

A strap on dildo, alternating ribs of gold and lapis lazuli, secured over her bone hips with leather thongs. It stood nearly two foot long.

The mummy of the nightmare queen was somehow still graceful despite the weight of the dildo, though her withered frame suggested her motions should have been stiff and jerking. She stepped from her sarcophagus with the ease of a woman emerging from a bath; in death her female curves had been replaced with the angles of awkward boyhood, an impression that made the withered flaps of her breasts and the insane sex toy she wore all the more grotesque. Her gold death mask was simple, lips curled in mockery, cheekbones high and haughty, eyes open and blind as a statue.

The pharoahess walked slowly towards him, her lithe gait at odds with the horror of her body, her strap on genitals swaying. Her step was so light that she could walk across the husk-bodies of her slaves without grinding them instantly to dust.

When she stood an arm's length in front of him she stopped.

She did nothing, spoke nothing.

The albino sniffed the air. She smelled of stale spices, dried onions. Dimly he recalled that when the heathen Egyptians prepared their dead in this manner they removed all the internal organs, including the brain, and stored them in jars. His senses told him this Vestal was different from the others; she was not formed from ectoplasm, but was in fact a walking corpse.

The nightmare queen of the Nile stood silent, waiting, waiting as she had done for uncounted centuries. Her dildo pointed to the center of his chest, whilst his own immense organ hung low and lazy between his thighs.

"Satisfy me," said the albino.

Her head tilted slightly to one side and a soft sound more the memory of a sigh than a sigh came from behind her mask.

He was not ready for what happened.

Her hands were at her sides one moment and in the next they were at his testicles and suddenly pain was his entire world. Her bone fingers were bands of iron that crushed his balls, and if he could have thought he would have understood that being not a creature of infernal vital-fluid the protective Enochian symbols tattooed onto his immense scrotum were no defence.

His fists sought her face by reflex, but her neck was of iron too and her mask took the blows without moving an inch. The albino bloodied his knuckles upon the gold and won no reprieve from his agony.

Her flesh on his flesh his inner eye opened and he SAW...

It was not just a simple pleasure toy no matter how lavish its materials the gold it was crafted from the precious blue stone it was ribbed with no not a mere plaything for the libido of an insatiable queen but in fact a holy relic of the heathens of ancient Egypt for contained within was the flesh of a god.

When the vision cleared he found himself emerging from the fog of pain to a dull ache as if he had been kicked in the stomach hard, over and over. His crotch was on fire and he found himself face down against cool stone.

Groggy, he started to push himself up, but a sharp foot was planted in the small of his back and he was once more forced to the ground.

The albino was unused to the position he found himself in.

Then something cold gently kissed his anus and he SAW...

Osiris the God of the Dead was killed by his brother Set who wished to usurp his throne and tore the corpse into pieces and scattered them until their sister Isis collected the pieces of Osiris together again except for his phallus which was lost and she fashioned a new one from gold and brought her brother to life again long enough to fuck him and bear his son Horus and the gold phallus became the secret treasure of the kingdom held by every ruler as a symbol of their power.

Then the gigantic dildo teasing the nerves at the mouth of his asshole shoved forward and over a foot of arm thick gold and jewelled dildo was forced up his anus.

Dry.

During his training there had been little work done on the reversal of roles during a sexorcism, and certainly it had been long since any demon had dominated him; the sensation of being violated made him scream. Bone and leather hands gripped his waist with terrible strength, preventing him from pulling away, stopping him from getting any leverage to struggle against her.

The nightmare queen made a sound that was something like the whir of scarab beetle wings and something like a crocodile hissing and the albino realized that she was laughing.

His rectum was stretched too wide, the unlubricated membranes burning, and he could feel the skin of his perineum pulled tight enough to split. His prostate was mashed tight and in spite of the pain in his balls he felt himself piss a hot jet of urine.

The mummy pushed more of the gigantic dildo into his ass and the ache in his balls was underlined by a sharp pain in his bowels like a shit held too long.

Clitocris pulled her hips back and the dildo slid partway out, the ribs scraping, until she swiftly punched it forward again and the albino felt *too much* go in and he vomited onto the stone floor his face was pressed against.

The buzz-hiss of her laughter was continuous as she raped him.

Somewhere deep inside himself away from the agony and the shame of being held down and violated by the immensely strong whore a single note of fear sounded; not given to emotions, particularly one as strong as fear, doubt was laid in his mind. Was this it? Was this how his duty was to end, fucked to death by an undead queen? She was surely too strong for him. He had no hope of overpowering her.

But these thoughts were short lived as he discovered that he was... aroused. His cock was stiffening swiftly, pressing against the rough stone floor and rubbing gently as his ass was rocked back and forth by the titan sex toy coring out his backside, the lapis lazuli ribs running back and forth across his prostate. He moaned into the bile he had spewed up, and knew he was once more in danger. Worse than pleasure, this was pleasure of the wicked sort.

Clitocris buzz-hissed and one hand let go of his waist long enough to spank his buttocks twice like he was a bucking colt. Then the hand plucked the Crucifux from the holsters bouncing on his thighs and threw them clattering amongst the bodies of her harem.

Even the loss of his own sacred sex toys did nothing to quell the building excitement in him, the familiar and yet forbidden rush of...

Just as he felt himself approaching that point where no man can pull themselves back from blowing their fuck no matter how hideous the circumstances he was stopped because somehow impossible Clitocris wearing the mythic phallus of the God of the Dead was coming. A pint of ice cold semen was being pumped into the albino's ass and his sphincter puckered closed but to no avail, the pressure was too great, the frozen spunk rushed up into his colon and further, cooling the boiling pain in his guts.

It felt incredible, but he did not come, by some miracle he did not orgasm in mindless pleasure; the coldness caused his balls to contract the way a dip in a freezing river would, and nipped his inner tubes tight against blowing his own fuck.

A bone finger pressed into the nape of his neck and then dragged down the length of his spine, and as it traced his backbone she pulled the giant dildo out of his ass with a vacuum-tight sucking.

THE WHOREHOUSE THAT JACK BUILT

The sensation of the enormous golden phallus being dragged out of him was like taking the biggest shit of his life... and as if it were a trigger, as the tip slid out of his stretched anus he felt his bowels release and thin slurry mixed with cold semen and blood gushed out of him.

He slumped to the floor, his hips no longer held up by the prop rammed up his guts, his belly splashing into piss, his face smeared across vomit, and thin faeces pooling between his legs.

He struggled to get his breath, trying to center himself, but his mind and his soul were out of spin. The albino had been raped before, but that did not mean he was hardened to it. Nobody could be; it was like being murdered, except there was no end in darkness. You were still alive after it was over.

He felt a hand of ivory sheathed in cracked leather grip his shoulder and flip him onto his back so easily he might have been as hollowed out as she was.

Clitocris was standing up, but she quickly grabbed the albino's still stone-thick penis and stood legs apart above his waist and lowered herself onto it, the dry, puckered, rough mouth of her desiccated anus scraping around the head of his erection. Helpless, he did nothing as she slid down onto him, gaining her knees and then sinking further until she was straddling him.

It was like tree bark or oyster shells were being scraped down the entire length of his shaft, so tight and dried out was her back passage, but perhaps worse still was the sensation that greeted him on the other side of that orifice. Her insides had been scooped out into jars so that her cavity could be seasoned with sawdust and dried herbs and preservative spices... but she was empty even of those things, and his cock pushed up into hollowness.

Lying on his back amidst the corpses he was looking at her death mask above the waving, filthy dildo, streaked with his blood and her semen, and in her hollowed out torso his erection waved in musty darkness; she shifted her weight and he felt her spine along the bottom of his shaft, before she shifted again and something thumped against the very tip of his bell end.

(there's something still inside her)

Clitorcris leant forward and grabbed his shoulders, pulling him up into a sitting position, bringing his face up to her mask; their body's separated by the titan dildo that reached their lips.

The blind eyes of her mask kept their secrets. Behind the cruelly smiling lips she rasped, a growl of desire from a dead throat; with a creak of ligaments she began to move up and down on him, his cock scraped going in and coming out of the crusty, flaky, dried pucker of her asshole.

The albino moved fast, unwrapping his rosary from one hand and whipping it around her throat and tightening the grip.

He knew it was futile to choke her; not only did she not require air, but the blessed metal had no effect on her either. Symbols of the faith would have no power over one who died three thousand years before the Nazarene did. But then he began pulling the rosary back and forth as hard and as fast as he could.

He knew he could not throttle her... but perhaps he could saw her fucking head off.

The Vestal Whore smacked his face so hard she loosened teeth, and as the albino gasped she gripped the back of his head and forced his mouth down around the end of her strap on sex organ.

This was more familiar to the albino. The Sisters all demanded regular servicing, so it was an automatic reaction for him to start working the golden shaft, his tongue flicking across its tip as his hands wrapped around the length and began to work the bloodshitty metal as if it were flesh.

The whore made a noise different to the mock hisses and buzzing sounds she had so far made; from vocal chords without lungs came a sound the albino recognized as pleasure.

Did the nightmare queen experience sensations through the sex toy?

The albino squeezed hard and gave two strong jerks on the filthy metal.

The dead throat sounded a deeper note. It seemed it was true that Clitocris could feel through the proxy prick.

He could buy himself time, work out a stratagem, if only he kept her distracted.

With all the skill he had he began to work the dead God's phallus in earnest, long and strong strokes up and down its length, fingers massaging the detailed art of the goldsmith who had worked in a pattern of swollen veins, even as he lipped and tongued the bell-end, drooling into the gasping mouth at the tip and then sucking his own saliva out again.

The pharoahess made noises very much like the purrs of a cat.

The albino's mind worked swiftly. The same as with each Vestal Whore before he had demanded satisfaction, and yet here he found himself working for her; he saw it as a diabolical reversal, a cunning ploy to wear him down. And it was still within the terms of the agreement, of course, as he knew there was a type of man who would consider the exchange of power in this situation to be entirely the definition of sexual satisfaction, the type of man who wanted to be brutalized and humiliated. He had not stated his actual preferences, and so had been offered the favours the disgusting, the obscene, the freakish, as there were men who would have deemed each of those previous Vestal's Whore's specialities as their carnal paradise... and now this, sucking his own blood and shit off the titan cock of a false God worn by a dead monster.

He had been trained to be the fucker, not the one being fucked. His anus was already a raw-ruin; how much more abuse would his body take before he forfeited it?

His only hope was to locate the undead queen of the Nile's Gash fast.

His fingers ventured under the enormous sculpted testicles of the dildo and searched out her perineum; he felt his own chafed shaft for a moment before she plunged herself down on it, and let his fingertips move forward. Vain hope though it was, he found a gap between the strap-on and her crotch and explored it, but found her cunt as dry and lifeless as her rectum.

Clitocris hissed, and began to bounce up and down on him even faster. His erection, sore as it was, wagged inside her hollowed torso, and again knocked against something.

(inside her knocked something like her chest is a bell with a clapper swinging)

THE WHOREHOUSE THAT JACK BUILT

The albino spat on the dildo and ran his tongue around and around the bell-end, turning his head to do so and snatching a glance at the mummy whore. The death mask was whipping from side to side and for moment he considered if the Gash might have been beneath that disguise, perhaps splitting her from forehead to chin, bracketed by empty sockets, an idea suggested by the stitching that ran from her crotch to her throat from where she had been cut open and eviscerated, ready for the tomb.

Still sucking, still rubbing, the albino frowned, realizing that the stitching did not match the age of the rest of the nightmare queen; it was surgical catgut, and fresh.

Not stopping to think, the albino increased his efforts, wrapping his mouth around as much of the dildo's enormous head as possible and sucking at it hard, hard, hard, one hand wrapping around the slick shaft and rapidly pumping the metal meat as his other hand slid around her hip, searching. Distracted by his mouth Clitocris paid no mind to the exploring digits that followed the strap-on's leather harness.

He found a knot, a simple one, easily tugged and loosened...

The whore stiffened and for a moment he feared he was discovered, but then a hideous rattle sounded in her dead throat and it was obvious she had stiffened in the same way a man does before he blows his fuck, and she blew hers, the God's artificial phallus again filling with nearly frozen seed and gushing into the albino's mouth in thick and potent spurts. It had the texture slug slime and was as strong and sour as vinegar. The albino swallowed the slime as fast as he could, but the flow was so strong it soon flooded his sinuses and jetted from his nostrils.

He felt his stomach filling, cramping around the icy sourness.

Then he was choking and he panicked, the gluey mess plugging his nostrils and clogging his throat, and he bucked against Clitocris hard enough to knock her backwards, bending his cock inside her and then she was slide-scraping off him, distracted by her own orgasm and the strap-on was unloosed from her hips and slid off as her nearly weightless body was pitched backwards.

The albino flopped over and coughed hooted and wheezed, eyes filling with tears, anything to dislodge the dead God's spunk, to breathe.

When he finally could breathe again he took great whooping lungfuls and waited for the attack, knowing that on his knees and feet he was vulnerable, once again presenting his anus to the whore. But the assault never came, and gradually he risked a glance over his shoulder.

Clitocris was lying on one hip and was trying to get up. But she was feeble, her former vigour gone. The albino saw the gold dildo lying on the ground between them and understood instantly; it was that which had made her strong, lent her corpse its power. He had pulled it off in his panic, and like Samson shorn of his hair, now its owner was powerless.

The mummy was trying to sit, reaching for the strap-on sex toy with one claw like hand, her mocking death mask now at odds with her insect-feebleness.

The albino staggered to his feet, turned on his heel, and kicked the phallus away with the side of his bare foot.

Then he grasped his cock, already hardening, and managed to imitate the sly sneer of the nightmare queen's gold visage.

"My turn," he muttered.

(something still inside)

He pressed his foot down on her left thigh, pinning her to the ground; her bony fingers scraped harmlessly at his calf. He leaned his weight down and grabbed her left ankle. Then he broke her leg at the knee like a dry tree branch, making kindling.

Clitocris hissed. Did she still feel pain?

The albino hoped she did.

Her broke her other leg. He broke her right arm, snapped it at the elbow, and finally broke the last of her limbs so that the mummy could only move her head.

Then he stomped on her chest and it was like stomping on an empty, dried out gourd; her ribs provided no resistance and the skin of her torso shredded like paper alongside either side of the new stitching.

Her head wagged back and forth and still she hissed.

The albino did not care. He reached down and pulled her ruined chest open.

Inside, hanging like the clapper of a bell in her hollowed out body, dangled her heart, hanging by its arteries. It was shrivelled as the rest of her; if the arteries were roots, it could have been a potato forgotten in the larder, having grown and ultimately died and become preserved.

But across its surface there were living lips. The Gash.

The albino squatted and tore Clitocris' ancient heart free of its mooring and standing impaled it on his cock, nearly ripping it apart as his erection burst through the leathery chambers. He stood like that for a moment, his cock throbbing with his own heartbeat, seeming to animate that which had stopped countless centuries before.

Then he squatted down again and pulled the death mask from the mummy's face.

With his hands holding the heart, cupping it, he began to saw his hips and intone;

"Lorem ipsum dolor sit amet," beneath the mask her skin and flesh were in the same near-ossified state as the rest of her body, "Consectetur adipisicing elit, sed do eiusmod tempor incididunt ut labore et dolore magna aliqua," except for her eyes, "Ut enim ad minim veniam, quis nostrud exercitation ullamco laboris nisi ut aliquip ex ea commodo consequat," they were young, and clear, and not demon eyes; they were human and beautiful and watching him with infinite hate, "Duis aute irure dolor in reprehenderit in voluptate velit esse cillum dolore eu fugiat nulla pariatur," and when the albino masturbated with the heart to the point of orgasm, "Excepteur sint occaecat cupidatat non proident, sunt in culpa qui OFFICIA deserunt MOLLIT anim ID EST LABORUM... AMEN" he made sure to blow his fuck in them.

The Gash died and finally the nightmare queen of the Nile died so long after her empire itself was dust.

CHAPTER VI

"Two beings had intercourse with Eve, and she conceived from both and bore two children. Each followed one of the male parents, and their spirits parted, one to this side and one to the other, and similarly their characters. On the side of Cain are all the haunts of the evil species; from the side of Abel comes a more merciful class, yet not wholly beneficial – good wine mixed with bad."

Zohar 136

"These are the generations..."

The secret catechism of the Order a series of questions and answers learned by rote and repeated as a mantra so that the questions and the answers became one.

In the Garden how many were there that went on two legs there were three that went on two legs Adam and Eve and the Other.

Who is the Son of God He is His own Son.

What was its name that was the Other the Other in the garden was called the Serpent.

Who was the mother of God the Virgin Mary was the mother of God.

It is written that Adam knew Eve but once, yet how many children she bore Eve knew Adam once, but she bore two children.

And who was the wife of the Son of God the Whore Mary was His wife.

For whom did she bear the first child for the third in the garden?

And why was Mary Magdalene both his mother and his wife so as to keep the line Pure of the taint of the Other.

What was the name of the first child the first son of the Serpent was called Cain the Murderer and his son is Man whose line is tainted.

And so the Blessed Mary Magdalene the Virgin Whore was the mother and the wife of the Son of God, who was His own Son as only the Sacred Sin of incest has kept God's line Pure of the taint of the Serpent…

That was the secret the Order were charged with, that all of Mankind was descended of the Serpent, the Dragon, and the Devil; hadn't God sent a Flood to wipe them out? And hoped to save only Noah and his Family to repopulate the Earth? What of the recurrent wife-sister narratives of Genesis, veiled references to hieros gamos, of Lot's daughters seducing him after the fall of Gomorrah…

"These are the generations…"

The Order of the Immaculate were descendants of a line of inbreeding begun in the Garden and carried on the Ark and into Egypt and continued down secretly through the ages even as the

THE WHOREHOUSE THAT JACK BUILT

Serpent's family swarmed in greater numbers, flourishing no matter how He flogged the Earth —by Flood, by Fire, by Plague— providing the flesh and blood to fuel the engines of Hell...

*

The final nightmare loped through the darkness towards him.

His body stinking of every human waste he stood in dim twilight and steeled his will so that it might lend iron to his rod one last time. His face and his chest, his belly and thighs and hands were crusted and sticky with shit and semen, with piss and puke. He blinked through a mask of filth and when he flexed his fingers he felt gluey-webs between his knuckles.

He was stood in a cavern dimly lit by phosphorescent fungus, tumescent toadstools that clustered the roof like cancerous growths. The cavern could have been in the roots of one of the great mountains that spanned the untamed expanse of the Pacific North-West. It was twenty yards side to side and half as tall, and at the further end it narrowed down to a throat, a deeper cave that contained utter darkness and the sound of something approaching.

Something huge.

At first when he had stepped into this room that was not a room he had been unaware of the sound as a sound but gradually as his eyes adjusted to the gloom he had felt it in his gut as a steady rhythm of footfalls like the war drums of savages, closing rapidly, until finally he heard it as well as felt it stumbling up through the darkness towards him from unimagined depths of the earth.

There were primitive paintings on the walls. The albino did not look too closely at them for not only their extreme age disturbed him but also their subject. One glance at the shadowed work on the walls showed not hunting scenes but instead beasts like buffalo and strange hairy elephants being raped by giant man-shaped figures. And the artist approached...

The sound of loping footfalls slowed and slowed and then finally stopped and it stood still in the deeper darkness of the cave mouth, just beyond the dim light of the outer cavern.

He could feel its gaze on him; hear the steady thunder of its breathing. He could smell it, and the smell was disturbing; it was the scent of a woman on her fertility cycle, only to the tenth power; meaty and spiced and sour and sickening even as it excited. The reason for the stench was apparent in the next moment, for that which lumbered into the fungus lit cavern was pregnant.

Human shaped and ten feet tall, every inch of flesh covered in filthy pubic hair that seethed with lice and millipedes, crusty-matted fur all flesh except for pendulous breasts and the titanic cunt that split it almost from asshole to navel beneath the barrel swell of its belly.

The albino looked up at the demon's face, almost entirely obscured by louse riddled hair. Deep set black eyes, that was all that peered through, the rest of her features lost in curly, clotted fur; he couldn't even see a nose or a mouth, only hair. A beast and yet its eyes flashed with intelligence. In silence it stared at him.

He had spoken with mountain men as he hunted the Half-World, and sometimes they told of demons in the far forests, on lonely peaks, man shaped only far larger than any human. Pelt traders and prospectors who knew scripture muttered of the world before the Flood, "*Giants were on the earth in those days, and also afterward...*" The Indians knew of these giants, and avoided their mountains and forests, called them the Old Ones, Kwi-kwiyai, Sasquatch.

"Ginger" was a Sasquatch. He had fucked women and men and children and animals and corpses in his years of training and in his duties wherever they took him he had sexorcised countless devils of every disgusting breed but the creature stood before him was something entirely other. If God's line had been kept pure through the miracle of incest, then surely here was proof that the Serpent, that Other who had walked in Eden, had also kept a scion of its own preserved through the ages.

It was nearly twice his size. One of its hands could form a fist around his skull. And somehow he had to fuck it to extinction.

The albino gripped his cock and began to work it hard.

The giant called Ginger watched, her eyes still peering from behind a fringe of filthy red-brown hair, one of her huge, fur matted hands instinctively cradling her belly in a gesture that was all too human.

The albino stepped forward, peggo rising in his grip, swelling with lust and spunk.

With a grunt the Sasquatch stooped forward and used its free hand to swat him back, fast for its size, the back of her hand smacking his chest and sending him flying back a yard and a half onto his bare backside on the cold dirt floor of the cavern. Winded, the albino had no time to recover before Ginger was stooped over him, crouched at his side and looking down like he was some interesting insect crawling across the ground. She stared into his eyes for a moment, gusts of foul breath blowing from the tangled mess of fur that obscured most of her face, and then she turned her attention to his crotch.

The albino tried to sit up, but she pushed him down again with a finger tap to his chest that felt like being punched, a single finger the same size as his cock and his cock was being gripped by another finger that huge on her other hand, a finger and a colossal thumb that pinched his meat lightly and gently jerked at him, as if testing to see how deeply it was anchored in his guts, as if to rip it out by the artery-roots. Most people could barely wrap their hands around it, let alone pincer it between two fingers.

Then the Sasquatch's grip became softer, almost gentle, and she frigged his cock lightly, the bell end bulging huge and shiny stretched tight with blood. The albino felt a groan building in his gut but held it; he had almost lost himself to pleasure too often already. He wouldn't lose sight of his duty for a simple hand job.

Then her whole hand engulfed his genitals and Ginger stood up and she did not let go and with a sickening lurch the albino was hauled up to hang by his manhood from the Sasquatch's grip.

If the albino hadn't been so scrawny and his cock had not been so huge he might have been emasculated instantly, but instead of having his genitals torn from his body he found himself crucified in mid-air by an experience entirely novel to his extensive experience. He had been hung by the neck before of course for the act of erotic asphyxiation, and suspended in any number of torture devices adapted for carnality, but finding his back arched and his arms and legs swimming in open space as the creature lifted him higher and higher...

The novelty was only matched by the agony. Though his flesh did not give, it burned as though it might rip asunder at any moment, his skin splitting with a wet crackle of membrane and erectile tissue being torn under his weight.

She bounced him up and down, lightly, as if he were a child's toy, a yo-yo. The sensation was extraordinary; at every jerk he felt as though he might be castrated, but still he felt gobs of pre-come squirting up his shaft.

He found himself upside down but eye to eye with the Sasquatch, holding his cock high above her head to dangle him in front of her face. She sniffed him.

Then Ginger opened her mouth.

Previously concealed under the heavy hair that matted her entire face, her mouth seemed to split her whole head open; the albino thought of a snake eating an egg much larger than itself, the jaw unhinging and swinging impossibly wide.

Except the Sasquatch's mouth was not horizontal, but *vertical.* It was like a pussy lined with teeth.

He cried out against the sight, swung his fists uselessly, but in the next moment his entire head was in her mouth. Her teeth were a choker high around his throat even as moist darkness smothered his face. Then she sucked; she sucked deeply on his head like it was a pebble to prevent against thirst in the desert, and the albino felt the saliva pulled from his mouth and the wax deposits out of his ears and the snot from deep in his sinuses and he clamped his eyes shut because the suction threatened to pull them from their sockets.

He came, blessed seed gushing in an ivory fountain of salty tallow from his rainbow hued agonised erection.

Ginger let go of his spurting erection in shock and his body dropped almost breaking his neck and for a moment he dangled between her lips and he thought she was going to bite. Then her hands were on his shoulders and he thought of a painting by Goya, *Saturn Devouring His Children*, and then he was out of her mouth gasping cool cavern air but the sasquatch was not done with him she was licking all over his body lapping up the crusts and filth caking him handling him like a doll or a

(childe)

newborn animal, her tongue as huge as two hands steepled in prayer slapping wetly against him.

The albino did not struggle now, his body relaxing, knowing best, that to resist would be pointless. The beast was a Vestal Whore, and no matter how bizarre its behaviour it would not kill him. Not before...

The cavern span about his head and the albino was being held by the hips and lips were wrapped around his rump and then the Sasquatch was sucking again tongue teasing his anus for a moment before it slurped god-semen and dildo-packed shit out of his rectum.

He was no stranger to a tongue in his ass, but being eaten out was rare. The albino's confusion grew, even as the only explanation of Ginger's behaviour occurred; she was cleaning him. Animal instinct. The way a mother cat washes her kittens, for some reason the Sasquatch was cleansing him, having licked the dirt from his body and even sucked the filth from his orifices.

THE WHOREHOUSE THAT JACK BUILT

Perhaps her maternal instincts were confusing her.

It was some minutes after this bizarre activity had begun that the albino found himself upon his own feet again, the saliva of the beast drying on his skin. His head spun, the root of his cock ached from being lifted bodily by it and he was covered in bruises from the sasquatches handling of him, but otherwise he was as clean as he had been upon first entering the Half-World.

The Vestal Whore Sasquatch stood back from him, one hand gently rubbing the enormous swell of her belly. She could have been pregnant with a mule; such was the size of her. Then she gently lowered herself to the dirt floor of the cold cavern and laid herself down, her great long back rolling out across the ground until she was laid almost flat, propping herself on one elbow to look back at the albino over the swell of her belly... and parted her legs wide.

Of course. A creature from a hidden race she might have been but also a whore she was, and there were many whore's who insisted on their customers bathing before they made the beast with two backs.

She was supplicant, her dark eyes watching impassively from the extreme end of her enormous body, peering over the fur matted bulge of her pregnancy that lead suddenly down between giant hairy thighs to the engorged lips of her sex, a cunt vaster than that of any animal he had ever seen or fucked.

One of her huge, human like hands slid over her left thigh and the thick fingers spread her lips apart to show him the perverted miracle of her for she was big with childe and yet still a virgin.

Her hymen was intact. Perfect. Untouched.

The albino's whole being was shaken, as a candle flame disturbed by the beating of great wings in the darkness. His mouth ran dry and his heart beat a dangerous tattoo as before him was a twisted version of the Sacred Sin waiting to be committed.

His erection ached as hard as it had ever been longing and lust twin serpents that seemed to twine around its length and squeeze his cock whose skin was every colour of the prism in memory of the first covenant and mutilated in accordance with the second his cock that had pleasured and killed often at the same time finally in the presence of a cunt haughty enough to take all that it might give.

The albino fell upon the beast, arms flung over her hairy hips, securing himself between her furred thighs even as he drove his loins forward and he shoved the length and the girth of himself into hot juice and pungent meat that welcomed him into its depth.

Flesh on flesh.

Hail Mary...

He SAW.

But that first impression was not a vision from life but instead a feeling like the little death, what the French call the moment of orgasm, the moment when the self is extinguished and on entry did the albino feel himself annihilated.

No ego. No past. No self. No future. No hope. No desire.

Free.

He came too to find his hips on reflex, pumping his cock back and forth in the enormous cunt even as red eyed things half-barnacle and half-slug oozed out of Ginger's filthy pubic hair to

THE WHOREHOUSE THAT JACK BUILT

hiss and nip at him with slimy crab-mouths. Such was his ecstasy that he paid their bites no mind; demons had venereal parasites almost as varied and repellent as themselves.

His duty was forgotten; all that was left was the animal part of his nature, the rutting beast of the fields. But even as he thrust wildly a frustration grew in him; his grip was secured by his hands wrapped in her dirt fur, but he was not secure at the waist.

Her cunt was *too* big.

Even as huge as his organ was still he found too little friction, too little grind. He slipped and slid about in her, where with every partner he had had before he had found himself plumbing tightness, often such tightness that his cock would rip apart whatever orifice it was stuffed into. But not here.

With no firm grip, a cock can never mount towards release.

He howled his frustration; Ginger also seemed aggrieved, as apish fingers appeared between him and her sex to expose her engorged clitoris and rub frantically against it.

The albino renewed his efforts though without hope, a mechanical process that only confirmed the dilemma and soon he found himself pushing away from the giant's crotch, stumbling back between the spread of her legs and looking down at his frustrated erection with something close to shame as between Ginger's thighs, between the folded curtains of flesh which were too much even for God's own sexorcist, the sasquatch's virginity was still intact.

Ginger was making strange coughing sounds.

He had not even broken her hymen.

She was not coughing.

The albino glanced up to see her peering over her pregnant belly, eyes full of mockery. No, she was not coughing; she was laughing.

He'd been humping her inner lips and hadn't entered her at all. His cock had failed to pierce her, had slid off and left him rutting the groove of her labia minor.

And she laughed at him.

It was the ultimate mockery. Since had had come to the Americas he had sexorcised the Manhattan chapter of the Hellfire Club and had fucked to unlife the voodoun fetish-bitches of the Cafe L'Enfer in New Orleans... but to have failed to have deflowered this beast who was a perverted mockery of the Virgin Birth... a simple New World demon who now mocked him...

Hail Mary full of grace...

He had no idea of what he was to do before suddenly he was doing it. A dervish he became; a Crucifux in his hand he plunged between the sasquatch's thighs, hissing back at the barnacle-slug parasites which reared up in her pubic hair, almost diving into her genitals, sacred dildo stabbing before him to rip through the skein of tissue that mocked him, mocked the truth of her swollen belly. The sex toy carved of the true cross pierced the hymen and split it in a welter of blood that drenched his arms and face and chest

(if a bear could scream such was the sound the sasquatch made)

he threw the Crucifux aside and plunged his right hand into her cunt, his razor/rosary wrapped fist punching in, sank in her up past his forearm, his elbow sliding in, his anger and shame and frustration lending him lunatic purpose, all the lessons learnt to quash his emotions utterly discarded now. He felt the Sasquatch's hands at his back, but he was slick with blood and wriggled free of her clumsy fingers.

HAIL MARY FULL OF GRACE.

The rosary lacerated her insides, making her screech. He shoved his arm in deeper, fingers probing deeper, groping, breathing in hot copper as blood flowed, taking a lungful of air and then plunging his face in as well, somehow sliding his whole head in after his arm, one shoulder even squeezing in as his strong right hand ventured further, deeper, razor-rosary ripping and slicing, blood, blood, blood, lubricating...

Flesh on flesh he SAW...

In the mountains and the ancient forests vast and quiet where no human had ever been her tribe lived in peace for unknown generations eating what the land gave them and never wanting more knowing nothing of desire and the suffering that was its twin living and dying without names.

His fingers found something and it moved like a snake. On instinct he grabbed it, grabbed it as hard as he could, blood/slick, blood slippery, and began to pull.

(Eden this was the Garden this was what the stories really meant to be an animal without knowledge of Self a part of the world and not separated from it by the illusion of Self and the nonsense that attended it..)

Her hand found his leg, long fingers wrapped around his thigh, and as she pulled he pulled and the bear-screaming was loud even with his ears muffled by the bloody walls of her pussy.

Then the Little Ones came across the land bridge of the West and they drove the tribe deeper into the mountains and forests and the tribe learned to avoid the Little Ones who wore the skins of animals and burned their food but the Little Red Skinned Ones were not the worst for in their own way they were barely more than animals themselves the worst would come centuries later when the land bridge of the West was gone and the Little White Ones came from the ocean of the East and brought their God with them.

The albino gasped as his head was pulled free, inhaling the cold cave air greedily, lending fresh oxygen to his muscles that then tightened and pulled harder still even as he felt his leg being nearly pulled from his hip socket.

A God who knew They would Fall a sadistic monster who made a world of Desire & Agony. Who made Adam? Who made Eve? Who made the Serpent, put lust in its breast and loins, set in motion the creation of a world where everything yearned to fuck and fucking was a sin and being born was a sin and a punishment the punishment that new life must be born in agony. This was the punishment only humans knew; the beasts of the fields knew not themselves nor desire nor agony.

He flipped upside down as the Sasquatch lifted him aloft, still howling as she felt what was being done to her, what she was assisting; the albino's arms slid out of her cunt and then his hand, and that was gripped tightly around a length of rope that was not a rope. A wide mouthed face appeared drenched in gore, seeming to scream in time with its mother though no sound issued; the albino had caught the umbilical cord and that in turn had wrapped around the foetus's throat.

It looked almost human, the brood of swine and apes.

The albino wrapped his length of umbilical cord tight between his fists and jerked hard. The whole body nearly as big as himself slid out on a tide of amniotic fluid and blood and the afterbirth it was entwined with. Curled up, eyes closed, its slick furred limbs moved feebly as it tried to take its first breath.

The albino felt himself flung aside, tumbled through the air to hit the cavern's dirt floor in a tangle of arms and legs and flopping cock.

For a time he lay winded, fearing his leg had been dislocated in the violence. But apart from the pain it felt okay, he could move it. He breathed deeply, each lungful won at the expense of who knew how many fractured ribs.

The albino grew aware of a sound low and terrible.

He sat up, gasping at the pain, his cock nearly flaccid and a single dildo left in his gun holster. He had landed some dozen yards away from the Sasquatch, who was also sat up now, her body hideous in the way that females are after giving birth, somehow collapsed and misshapen.

She was cradling her child, urging its lifeless lips to a teat and making that low and terrible sound. She sat in a puddle of blood-mud, still bleeding from the abortion the albino had performed on her, and that sound she made was the start of a scream of sorrow and hatred he knew for he had heard it before.

Even demons could grieve.

When he tried to stand his choked sob of pain brought her head up and her eyes fixed his.

And then she screamed the scream that had been boiling up in her.

Her child was dead and she threw it aside, her eyes seething with insanity and never leaving the albino's face as her enormous mouth vented a bellow of horror and sorrow and hatred. She too began to stand, but even as she found her feet her legs buckled under her; the pool of blood that she had stood up from was the reason she was so weak. She toppled to her knees, fell to her hands and her scream became a groan as she rested heavily upon the floor of the cavern.

Her breathing was hard and harsh. She had lost so much blood, was still losing it. She was dying.

But her eyes never left the albino, who still could not stand.

And she began to crawl towards him,

Words came to the albino's mind, not words from any holy text, but rather from the most celebrated novel of Mr Melville;

"*To the last I grapple with thee.*"

He saw there was no reason in the creature's eyes, that her demonic bonds had been broken by something stronger even than the chains of Hell; the bond of mother and child was stronger.

The contract would be broken. He would not Know her. She would destroy him.

The albino did not try to escape her. He drew his second Crucifux.

One monstrous hand grabbed his ankle. Her strength was flowing out between her legs, but her will was set on her final act;

her vast mouth opened wide, rimmed with rotting teeth, and she dragged the albino towards her.

He lay flat upon his back, being dragged across the dirt floor, Crucifux clasped to his chest, and he set himself to pray.

No holy words came to his lips, but others.

"From Hell's heart," said the albino, "I stab at thee."

With a grunt he sat up, his ass dragging in the dirt, and found his foot already in her mouth, being fed in between her jaws ready to bite. The momentum of sitting aided his thrust as he rammed the tip of the divine dildo into her right eye as hard as he could, bursting it and smashing through the thin bone in the back of the socket to puncture the sasquatch's brain.

The effect was shocking in its swiftness. One moment the creature was about to devour him from the feet up, and in the next it dropped dead, lobotomised with a giant wooden cock.

He had done the same to Bear-Maiden, but that demon had kept going, made of erectoplasm. The Sasquatch died though; she was alive, real. Something rare had gone out of the world.

The mouth closed loosely around his calf as the head hit the floor, one eye still open and staring.

The albino was breathing heavily, his heart racing.

He had killed it. He'd killed the fifth Vestal Whore before he had fucked its Gash.

The albino pulled his foot free of the Sasquatch's mouth. For a moment a skein of thick saliva hung between his toes and its lips, and then broke.

Then he lay down to wait. His flesh, his blood, and his soul were all forfeit, for he had broken the contract. On reflection, being eaten alive by the Sasquatch would have been better; instinct had made him fight for his life, but if he had simply let himself be killed then at least his soul would have been saved. The deal was broken, and he was the offending party. The penalties did not bear thinking of.

He composed a prayer to Mary Magdalene, the Virgin Whore, mother and wife of the Nazarene. The nature of the prayer was not to ask forgiveness of his sins, but only to ask forgiveness for having failed.

He waited. Above him, the luminescent fungi hung in auras of their strange and sickly light. Auras, gloriole, the ring of light surrounding Heavenly visions; tears stood in his eyes, sorrow knowing there could never be forgiveness for such failure as his.

He expected the architect of flesh, expected gloating before ultimate darkness and an eternity as a plaything of Hell. Or perhaps McGregor's demon sponsor, the Arcimboldo, would personally come to collect such a prize as he; not only a holy man, but one of the Sons of the Order of the Immaculate.

He waited.

Nothing came to claim him

The albino did not understand. He sat up again, slowly, and looked at the Sasquatch. The Crucifux still protruded from the egg-glue mess of its right eye, a trickle of blood running down into the stinking pubic hair that covered its cheek. Its good eye was now fully glazed over and already a smell was coming from the flesh as it began to dissolve back into erectoplasm, a smell of rotting fish.

Warily the albino got up, hissing with pain at his assorted injuries, unsteady on his latest, the leg almost pulled from his hip.

THE WHOREHOUSE THAT JACK BUILT

He expected to be ambushed and so let no hope enter into himself as to allow hope and then suddenly have it snatched away would take his dignity too. This was Hell's way of business.

But there still was nothing.

He stood looking down at the long body before him, watched as parasites fled the growth of pubic fur that matted it, multi-segmented creatures twitching antennae and compound eyes and mandibles and egg sacs. Even the slug-barnacles oozed from the crust-sores around her cunt and started to ooze away from the dwindling warmth.

Some of the creatures headed instead for the other corpse.

The albino watched the parasites crawl towards the aborted Sasquatch and wondered stupidly why they did. And suddenly he had inkling.

He tottered unsteadily around Ginger's corpse and followed the parasites.

Why would they leave their dead host for another dead host?

They would not.

The foetus was breathing, alive. Being suddenly cast down by its parent had performed the same action that a mid-wife smacking an infant human will; it started the lungs breathing air for the first time. The umbilical cord had only choked it in the sense that its mother's oxygenated blood had been stopped in flow.

The parasite colonists swarmed the baby, but only so that they could lay clutches of eggs upon it before they died, leaving off-white bubbles knotted into its fine, still wet fur.

The albino stood over these new generations, and wondered. The infant sasquatch breathed quietly, its eyes still closed against the world like the newborns of many species, on its side with its arms curled to its chest and its knees drawn up, but not hiding what lay between them.

Between its legs it was male and female.

The final mockery. A virgin birth that aped the secret of the Order. A hermaphrodite, but not a true one. It was a creation of chirurgery after all; its tiny testicles and penis hung below the cunt of an adult, human female. The fifth and final Gash was in the infant's abdomen.

The albino felt himself hardening. Sticky with blood, the colours of his cock were turned almost black, a stain'd rainbow that began to arc and to arc and finally straighten out into the longest, hardest erection he had ever had, a forearm that rose from his groin with its giant fist clenched in triumph.

"This is how it is done," said the albino, winding the umbilical cord around his own throat and pulling hard on it, choking himself even as he impaled the baby sasquatch's Gash; it was the same size and weight as a three year old human, easily impaled and lifted on his crotch.

Then he fucked the baby Sasquatch to death.

"Lorem ipsum dolor sit amet, consectetur adipisicing elit..."

he sank up to his nuts in guts

(Mary Maggie Darling)

"...sed do eiusmod tempor incididunt ut labore et dolore magna aliqua..."

and further still he felt himself filling its throat

(Bear-Maiden)

"...ut enim ad minim veniam, quis nostrud exercitation ullamco laboris nisi ut aliquip..."

and up further into the brain

(Grandma Spuckler)

"...ex ea commodo consequat, Duis aute irure dolor in reprehenderit in voluptate velit esse cillum dolore eu fugiat nulla pariatur..."

his cock on its way through had shoved everything before it a meat piston pushed the creature's heart

(Clitocris)

"...excepteur sint occaecat cupidatat non proident, sunt in culpa qui OFFICIA deserunt MOLLIT anim ID EST LABORUM... "

up into its mouth and the tough knot of muscle bulged between its' lips like the apple in the mouth of a suckling pig and choking himself to the point where his eyes filled with bright flashes and black spots he came a flood a fountain a roaring torrent of hot salty sticky come so hard that the soft spot the fontanel on top of the baby sasquatch's head exploded like a gigantic boil spewing brain and semen.

Amen.

CHAPTER VII

(a great sign appeared in the sky)

he carried me away into the wilderness and I saw a woman

(a woman clothed with the sun)

sat upon a red dragon, full of names of blasphemy and the woman was arrayed in purple and scarlet colour

(with the moon under her feet, and on her head a crown of twelve stars)

having a golden cup in her hand full of abominations and filthiness of her fornication

(she was with child and wailed aloud in pain as she labored to give birth)

and upon her forehead was a name written a mystery Babylon The Great the mother of whores and abominations of the Earth

(another sign appeared in the sky it was a huge red dragon with seven heads and ten horns and its tail swept away a third of the stars in the sky and hurled them down to the earth)

and I saw the woman drunken with the blood of the saints and with the blood of the martyrs of the Savior and when I saw her

(then the dragon stood before the woman about to give birth to devour her child when she gave birth)

I wondered with great admiration

THE WHOREHOUSE THAT JACK BUILT

(she gave birth to a son a male child destined to rule all the nations with an iron rod)

*

A door opened.

Wearily, the albino staggered forth from the darkness back into the impossible giant room he had stepped into when first he crossed the threshold of the Half-World.

He looked about him and barely even saw the mansions that had once littered the vast wooden plain now collapsed into ruins of brick and board, their rutting occupants crushed. His eyes fell upon McGregor Marshall, sat upon the ground in front of him, surrounded by destroyed doll houses.

The dwarf was weeping, cradling dolls. Dolls that were instantly familiar, dolls whose stitches had been burst from which their stuffing was bleeding.

"Mah gels," he sobbed; his cock was flaccid now, and tiny, a new born bird crushed under the sweating rolls of his gut, "Ye fuckin' swine… ye cunt ye, ye wiped out mah gels. The Vestals…"

There was a distant roll of thunder.

"It's over," said the albino, "The sexorcism is complete."

And it was; each Gash had been fucked, been filled with his sacred seed, the product of generations of hermaphrodite inbreeding. Five keyholes that opened the way to the Abyss, that allowed the passage of flesh and blood into the infernal spirit world, had been broken.

The thunder rolled again.

His duster lay where he had discarded it and his smoked spectacles as well. He dressed slowly, his body protesting at all the abuses heaped upon it in the past few hours. Though he had been conditioned to put aside all thoughts but his duties, to suppress any ego he had, to be emotionless... he felt he deserved a feather mattress.

The thunder again; it was coming closer; across the wooden plain it came.

"Years!" screamed the dwarf, and his fists beat upon the ground, "Years ah spent preparing! The pacts ah made, the blood ah had to spill! And then ye came and ye *spoiled everything!*"

McGregor was pathetic and wept for himself. The eunuchorn guards who had stood at the door now flanked the magician, to prevent his escape, though such action on his part seemed unlikely. He more resembled a spoiled toddler in the last fits of a tantrum, a grotesque man-baby sat amongst toys he had destroyed in idiot rage.

A door stood open through which a prairie breeze blew. It smelled good. Clean. Pure. Without memory.

The thunder was closer, coming closer.

The albino gave the eunuchorns a wide berth, though they paid him little enough attention; their focus was elsewhere, their heads tilted up looking at something further off, behind him, in the approaching distance.

It was not thunder.

The albino made the threshold and was half in the world outside when like Lot's wife he glanced back.

Not thunder but footsteps.

THE WHOREHOUSE THAT JACK BUILT

A foot came down on the Half-World, crushing it as if it were a house of cards.

The Beast had come for the one who had failed it

(as above so below)

titanic McGregor looked like a doll it stooped to pick up

(goat eyes as big as cartwheels and they SAW)

flesh pure white apart from its cock which was as huge as a locomotive and was every colour of the...

The albino left then without witnessing what came next and when the door closed behind him it closed on a building that was just one more dead and deserted building in a dead and deserted town and saddled up his mule and he rode away into the evening redness in the West.

(and he or she had a cunt and was PREGNANT)

THE END

Also available from ~MorbidbookS~

In Print & Kindle Editions:

~click on image for HYPERLINK~

~Rae is her name. Our support group of embittered and most likely deranged women are going to kidnap, torture, disembowel and finally kill the woman who has ruined all our lives. As foul and as grotesque as she is, she acts like she's Queen of the Bean.

Rae, her buck-tooth grin and rosy cheeks of middle age acne reflected winter sun. Straw-like blonde hair obscured by the veil and tiara she enjoyed parading around in. She walked past our window with sickening confidence oblivious to us and our weak tea.

Rae. Everything was always about Rae. Was she a princess today, or was she a bride? Did she know or care? Did it even matter? We wished we could be that delusional and walk around with an air of not giving a damn. Rae believes she is above the pain she has caused. Beyond the whimpering of her victims. Out of reach of vengeance. Our support group of women do not agree. Judgement day is here for Rae.

~He didn't bother to undress—merely unzipping his pants and shrugging them down before dropping on top of her and entering her fiercely. His grunts as he thrust hard into her were loud and vulgar. She struggled and writhed violently beneath him.

"No! You will not move. You say I am a fucking clown, and so I will be. And I will fuck you until I can fuck you no more. And when I am done, perhaps I will take you down to the cattle car and watch while the other clowns fuck you one by one until you are so full that their juices run down your thighs."

Pinning her hands to the bed, he entered her quickly and roughly. She screamed and spit in his face. He slapped her again and left her ear ringing.

"You hate clowns? Well you have a clown inside of you right now. How does that feel? A fucking clown is raping you and he'll continue to do it until it pleases him to stop."

~Maybe it had started when he was at university.

He had a girlfriend in his final year that had gotten him into some weird stuff sexually then she left him for a guy with a bigger cock. The other guy was some gay looking chump with muscles and a tattoo; the pair had died in a car accident and Brian took a dump on their graves after each of their funerals. Fuck the both of them. But after she had left him he needed to fill the void of the newfound enjoyment of sickening sexual practices. Brain had purchased one of those 'real life' sex dolls online. Boy did the thing look real; you could bend it into any position and it came armed with enormous tits, willing mouth and a supposedly real feel pussy and anus. The packaging said to 'just add lubricant' but there was a problem. There was something missing; the smells, the tastes and the feel of real skin. You can't emulate that. So Brian set out to attempt to build a real life sex toy made from real life people.

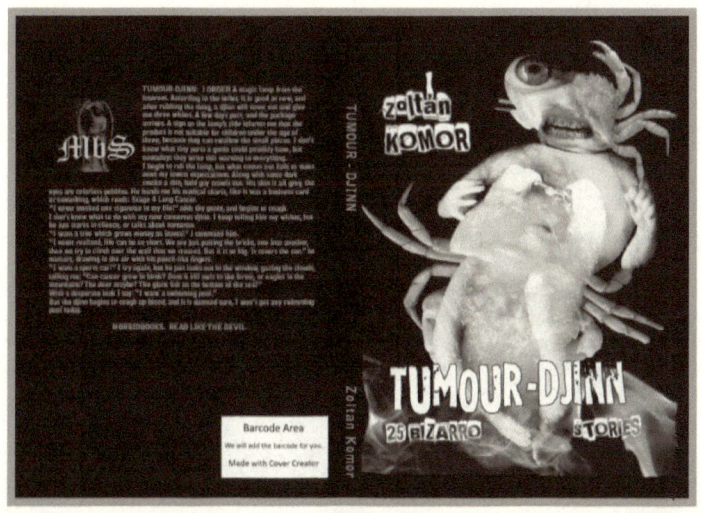

~I ORDER A magic lamp from the internet. According to the seller, it is good as new, and after rubbing the thing, a djinn will come out and give me three wishes. I begin to rub the lamp. Along with some dark smoke a thin, bald guy crawls out. His skin is all grey, the eyes are colorless pebbles.

"I want a tree which grows money as leaves!" I command.

"I never realized life can be so short. We are just putting the bricks, one into another, and then we try to climb over the wall that we created. But it is so big. It covers the sun." he mutters.

"I want a sports car!" I try again, but he just looks out in the window, gazing the clouds, telling me: "Can cancer grow in birds? Does it kill owls in the forest, or eagles in the mountains? The deer maybe? The giant fish on the bottom of the sea?"

With a desperate look I say: "I want a swimming pool."

But the djinn begins to cough up blood, and it is damned sure, I won't get any swimming pool today.

~**Keegan is a late-night public access radio show host,** sexual deviant, and militant vegan. He has grown tired of his vegan cause being treated with apathy by the portly, meat-gorging, residents of the small town of Breen Gay, Wisconsin.

The time is ripe for Vegan vengeance.

Keegan harvests roundworms from a local vagrant and mutates them using chemicals stolen from the meat packing plant. He infests the populace with the voracious, parasitic carnivores. Keegan knows that the only way for the people of Breen Gay to eliminate the parasites is to starve them of meat. It is with great expectation that he awaits the oncoming utopia of Veganism. However, the mutant roundworms will not die easily. The problems for the people of Breen Gay have only just begun.

~FOR SO LONG as anyone could remember, The Flagrant Five have ruled the land with an aggressive hand—enslaving children, destroying the wilderness—but Father Necrocious is tired of it all. One of his worst enemies (and a member of the Flagrant Five), Manservant Genesis, has escaped his imprisonment as a shadow.Therefore, he's enlisted the help of a ragtag group of fabricated Mercenaries to turn the fascists to shadows. The annual Dictators' Ball is pending (a battle in which children are used as pawns to determine the fate of the free world), and the brothers plan to stop the gala before it can commence. As they weave their way through the cartoonish landscape they will fight with their options to either trap the Flagrant Five with their shadow guns, or disobey their creator's orders and finally kill the Five for good.

~**The hands of the girls were inside of each–others zip front grey boiler suits** and they sat in the blood from where Sonny's face collided with the surface. The brunette had a finger smear of it next to her mouth.

"You two sluts put each other down and go tell Moira that Sonny's done. I'm coming in, just got a little business to attend to first."

As the two started to leave the big blond grabbed the shoulder of the red head and pulled her back.

"Not you Fire-Crotch, all this fucking blood has got me going." She started to unbuckle the belt on her camouflage hot pants. "Down you go, bitch!"

~**Short stories from the Most Depraved Writer in Print.** Dark and twisted tales of exquisite violence, rough tricks, narcotics consumption, evil ghosts and drug-snuffling demons. Evil grandfathers and animal-human hybrid clones. Morbid serial killer stalking night darkened hallways of an unsuspecting hospital. Life underground following the frozen apocalypse. Tales of ancient blood-thirsty vampires and Roman decadence. Enjoy all of the hardcore, dystopic, viscerally violent stories. Not for easily offended mamby-pambies. Dark fiction at its finest.

THE WHOREHOUSE THAT JACK BUILT

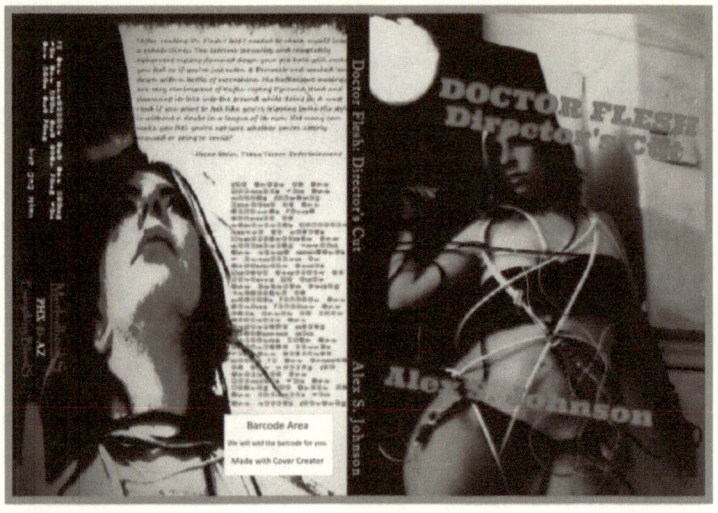

~From Alex S. Johnson, the author of Bad Sunset, Wicked Candy and The Death Jazz, comes a new vision in Bizarro horror. Imagine a TROMA film on meth and acid, one part cyberpunk, one part Franz Kafka, and three parts frankly unsuitable for a sane audience. "Will make you feel as if you've just eaten 8 Percocets and washed 'em down with a bottle of moonshine," says Necro Stein of Texas Terror Entertainment.

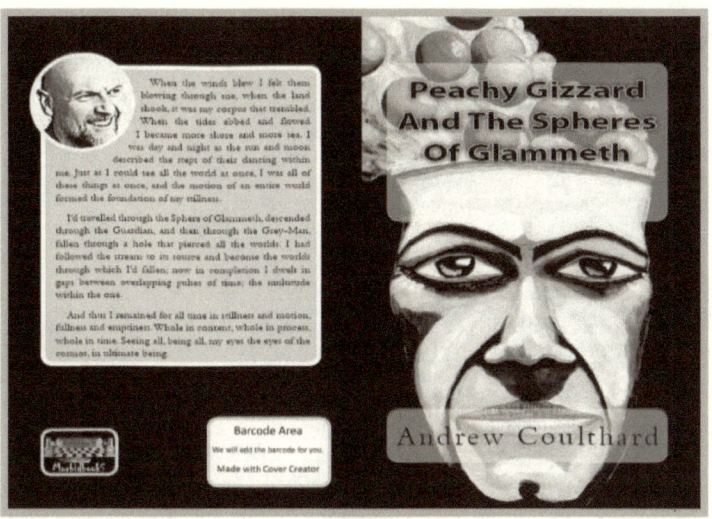

~**When the winds blew i felt them blowing through me,** when the
land shook, it was my corpus that trembled. When the tides ebbed
and flowed I became more shore and more sea. I was day and night
as the sun and moon described the steps of their dancing within
me. Just as I could see all the world at once, I was all of these things
at once, and the motion of an entire world formed the foundation
of my stillness.

I'd travelled through the Sphere of Glammeth, descended through
the Guardian, and then through the Grey-Man, fallen through a
hole that pierced all the worlds.

~**He had to have her the moment he saw her trachea ring**. Six months later she was his lovely wife. He performed his duties as a husband and she as a wife. He tolerated a house filled with references to her late first husband and the children they had together. He put up with her prudish ways. He waited. He was patient. He planned. He was adaptable. He was rewarded over the course of a week in her basement. He turned his perverse sexual fantasies of worms and maggots and her lovely crusty trachea ring into a gruesome reality.

~A dirty shameful devil of a secret...

Something that two men share. A legacy that will shock you to your very core. One that is created not out of madness, but of the purest desire. Take a vivid journey into the mind of the killer and his biggest fan. Do you believe in evil? See the knife plunge. Lap at the wounds. Do you still? There is no rational meaning or pretty words that will hide away the darkness that the words of this found journal creates. Inside is the real truth. And it can set you free. Watch all you want. Taste what you dare not have.

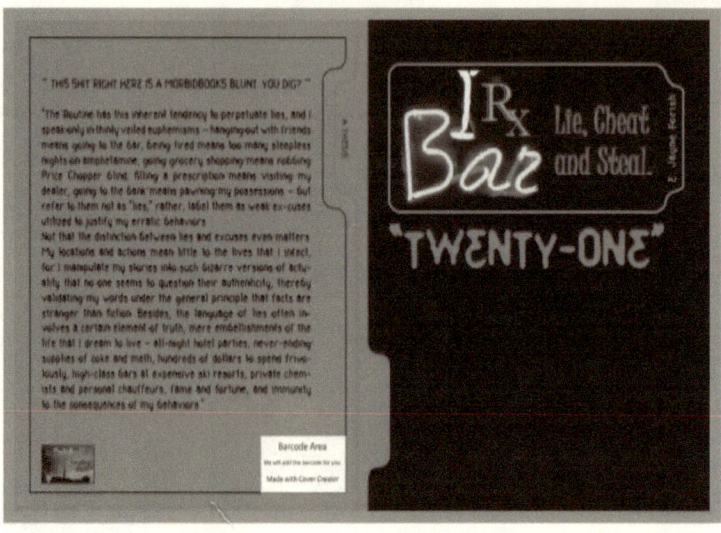

~"**The routine has this inherent tendency to perpetuate lies,** and I speak only in thinly veiled euphemisms — hanging out with friends means going to the bar; being tired means too many sleepless nights on amphetamine; going grocery shopping means robbing Price Chopper blind; filling a prescription means visiting my dealer; going to the bank means pawning my possessions — but refer to them not as "lies;" rather, label them as weak excuses utilized to justify my erratic behaviours.

~**I'm feeling down and dirty, feeling kind of mean,** so I give those fans my middle finger. Those poor bastards go nuts. My team looks at me in awe. My coach frowns and the opposing one begins to furiously scratch out new plays. I see our opponents and I almost feel sorry for the poor bastards. Their fans can't help them. Their coach can't help them. I'm going to run them off their own track in front of their own fans and there is not one thing they can do about it.

~**Humanity is the devil is a deconstructed nightmare mixing David Lynch and snuff movies.** The plot revolves around a central character, Seth, who is set about a crusade against humanity which, for him, represents pure evil. Through random killings he and his cronies try to accelerate the end of the world, in order to provoke and defeat the Demiurge, the false God that is ruling the earth. As in Burroughs, logical language is replaced here with cut-scenes – sometimes to be taken literally – that plunge the reader into an extreme experience.

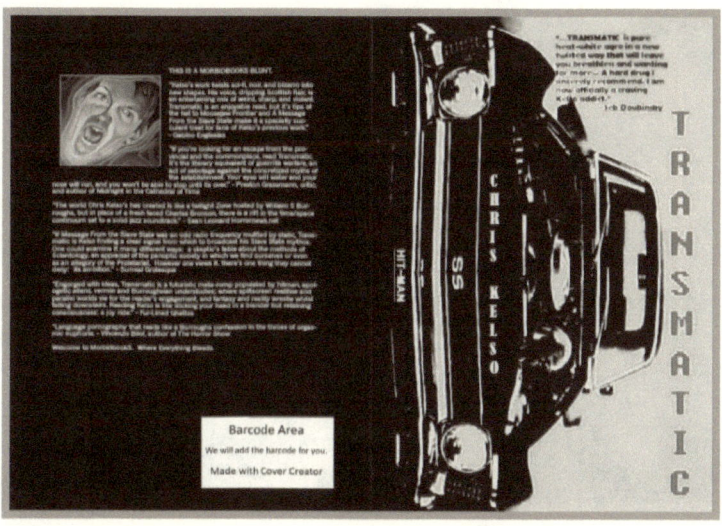

~"As a part-time hitman/ exterminator, Ignius Ellis's dream is to buy a candy-apple red Nova Supreme. In the process of trying to earn enough cash to make his dream come true he gets sucked into the rough world of Visitacion Valley, SF. When the tenants in his apartment complex reveal their various extracurricular activities this take an even more bizarre twist and Ellis soon becomes acquainted with the nightmarish Slave State dimension..."

~That's the last time she gets the bigger worm...

Once their flesh flakes away the angels collapse into puddles of hissing goop and withered petals blow into them hurried along by unseen winds. My spit looses its sweet taste to the black flavor of ash. The glowing birds in the bright orange sky burst into small sparkly novas. The sky itself weeps and tears, streaking down like a ruined painting as the dismal grey of life wheezes back before my eyes. I don't blink; praying silently for one last desperate sensation of the high. Lila feels it too. She writhes on the mattress next to me…

~Scary as ever.

He looked at her and grinned wickedly, the overcasting shadows of the outer corner of the stone wall, combined with the flickering light above them, created a deadly feature across the side of his face. He sees her lying helpless. He chuckled eerily, and instantly raised his hand. Her eyes widened to the sight of the gleaming sharp knife in his grasp. He even held it up for her to see it better. She stared up at him and then to the knife, panting in fear. Her heart pounded throughout her body as he chuckled once more saying deeply,

"Oh excellent. I've found you . . ."

~**Within these twisted and perverted pages**, Johnson manages to demolish clichés with a jaded finesse that I've personally never encountered in written form. Another apparent talent is his effortless deconstruction of pop-culture allegories and references as found in his story "Vampussy." No one is safe or spared from his dagger sharp sarcasm and wit.

While not without its flaws, my appreciation for this kind of talent and voice is what made his writing so fun to read, even if he might possibly be out of his ever-loving mind.

~In Garrett Cook's Murderland serial killers are idolized by society. Their deeds are followed obsessively by television pundits and the adoring public. A subculture has grown up around this phenomena, called "Reap." Laws are created to allow this activity to flourish, including designated "safe zones' where killers can practice their trade without fear of persecution. Fans of the top rated serial killers celebrate each new kill on social media and television. Programs glorify their deeds.

The culture of Murderland is violent and mirrors our own violent society and its decadent obsessions.

~**Born whole from the rectum of a dying patient, Morbid silently stalks the hospital's hallways,** heinously dispatching the most helpless of patients and in the most painfully repulsive of manners. In the meantime, in order to pay for his family and home that includes his ghost step-father Sammy and his pet aborted fetus Chip, Westphal has to ingest mounds of dangerous narcotics to get through his night shifts. Barely hanging on to his Care Tech gig by his fingernails, the last thing Westphal needs is to be accused of Morbid's evil deeds. You, on the other hand, simply seek some solace from all Your diseases.

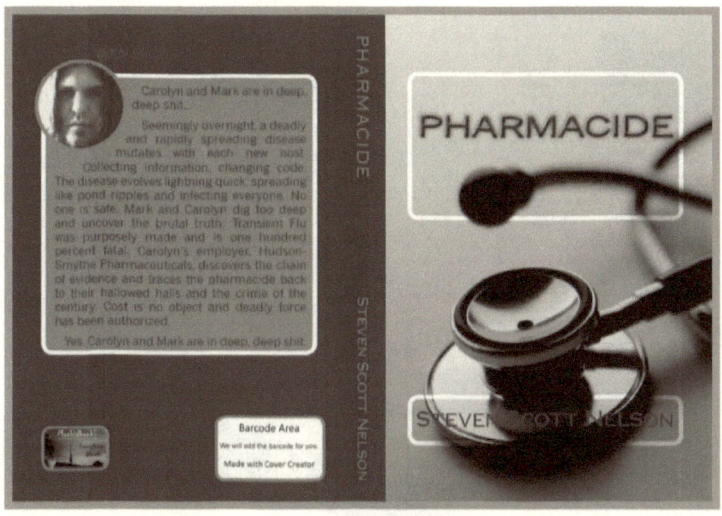

~**It looks like Carolyn and Mark are in deep, deep shit...** Mark and Carolyn live in an alternate 1989 where Ronald Reagan is on his fourth presidential term. The USA has a rigid, long-standing caste system and abortions were never made legal. Being homeless is a crime that is punishable by imprisonment in Tent City. Most of Mark's ER patients are inmates at this camp and are victims of a new disease dubbed: Transient Flu. This deadly and rapidly spreading disease mutates with each new host, collecting information, changing code. The disease evolves lightning quick, spreading like pond ripples…

~IMMANUEL THE CHRIST **has some nerve.** Jonah has already lost everyone he loves to Pilate the vampire and his Harbor drug violence. Jonah now trudges through his days staying as high on Plata as possible. He just wants to be left alone while he waits for his turn to die. The Christ has other plans for him. She sends Pedro, to assign Jonah to order the Herod to dismantle the Harbor's Plata trade. Jonah decides to run. But you can't run from God. As Jonah learns the hard way when the 'Edmund Fitzgerald' goes down in rough seas, with the reluctant prophet on board…

~**Five Very Wicked Shorts**. Brought to you with love and blood from The Grim Reverend Steven Rage, the 'Most Depraved Writer in Print'. ~

Through the sheer shock of his presentation, Rage forces readers to consider the alternatives, to look at the garbage in the streets, to see what is swept into the gutters at night right before all decent people awake to see another cleaned up version of the day. Depravity at its finest, but really the stories are loads of fun.

~Pontius Pilate is cursed to be a vampire. Life after life after life.~ And for the Plata dealing Pilate, his life is more like a death sentence. His only chance surviving is to keep on selling his monthly quota of Plata. This new man-made narcotic is a potent speed-ball designed to amp up the user, while also numbing the conscience into euphoric oblivion. To nullify the pain. To stifle the torture. To run and to hid from all the anguish inside. PILATE is a drug lord vampire in this re-telling of Christ's final days.

~So I, The Spun Monkey, have returned from running my errands, safe and sound. Having failed rehab once again, The Spun Monkey went ahead and procured myself an 8-ball of crispy, crunchy Columbian Bam-Bam. I chipped, chopped, lined and blasted off with two bigguns up each side. OOH OOH EEE EEE-fuckmerunning- OOH-OOH-OOH, motherfuckers! Monkey be ready... Yes, indeeeeeed.... Having had my jet fuel, I then sat my hairy asshole down at the keyboard and began flailing away. The monkey hopes you dig the fruits of my labors in 'The Spun Monkey's Digest'. And if you not ... well then ... you can go eff yourself, Capitan!

~**Following religious folklore, parables, and beliefs,** Rage presents the readers with a God who truly is the Shepherd that leaves no sheep behind. While this tale is deeply woven with the intricacies of a dark, drug-infested world ruled by evil forces, this is the story of a lost sheep. All are God's children, even the most foulest of evil creatures who by their own will have become so through their spiritual and physical copulation with the Devil, and as such, in God's mercy, still are given a chance to be saved.

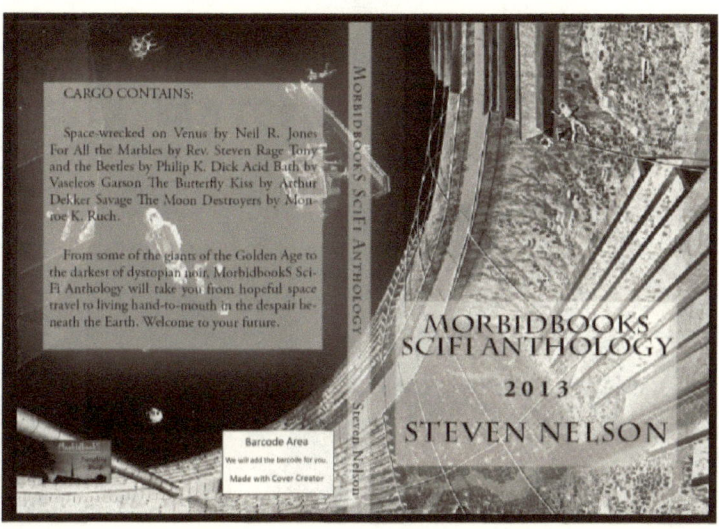

~ CARGO CONTAINS: ~

Space-wrecked on Venus by Neil R. Jones

For All the Marbles by Rev. Steven Rage

Tony and the Beetles by Philip K. Dick

Acid Bath by Vaseleos Garson

The Butterfly Kiss by Arthur Dekker Savage

The Moon Destroyers by Monroe K. Ruch

From some of the giants of the Golden Age to the darkest of dystopian noir, MorbidbookS SciFi Anthology will take you from hopeful space travel to living hand-to-mouth in the despair beneath the Earth.

Welcome to your future.

~**During the height of England's Bubonic Plague an ancient Evil Force strolls into London-Town** in the form of a would-be doctor. It could smell the blood from miles away, wanting only to help. At the hospital where he cares for the victims of this Black Death, the ill come to him unimpeded. They arrived and fell by the scores. With the help of his ever-faithful assistant, Sightless Agnes, a most ravenous cares for them all. Eating his way through an entire hospital, he treats them until there is nothing left. Nothing save their empty eye sockets, a few pounds of leeched bleached bones and some bolts of old dried-out flesh-leather parchment.

~**New from MorbidbookS: Where Everything Bleeds** is an instant collector's specimen and a certain stunner. ~ Be the first freak on your block to acquire this singular and unexpurgated exquisite culling of The Grim Reverend Steven Rage's favorite 'meds'. Enjoy this one-of-a-kind vivid look into the twisted mind of The Most Depraved Writer In Print as he captains you through the intoxicating stain of his wicked imagination. Included are numerous Photos, Paintings and Illustrations embellished with dramatic grayscale that enhance these iniquitous and magnificent Dark Fantasy fables.

~CLICK ON IMAGE FOR MORE MORBIDBOOKS ON KINDLE~

www.ingramcontent.com/pod-product-compliance
Lightning Source LLC
Chambersburg PA
CBHW021105130626
46554CB00002B/535